ACROS

'*Spoiled rich brats are just not my line,*' Dr Marc
Gérard tells Carla Younger at their first encounter.
How can she convince him that she is not just a social
butterfly when the mere fact that she abandoned her
nursing career only fuels his antagonism?

ACROSS THE PEARL RIVER

BY

ZARA HOLMAN

MILLS & BOON LIMITED
London · Sydney · Toronto

First published in Great Britain 1983
by Mills & Boon Limited, 15–16 Brook's Mews,
London W1A 1DR

© Zara Holman 1983

Australian copyright 1983
Philippine copyright 1983

ISBN 0 263 74201 6

03/0283

Set in 10 on 12 pt Linotron Times

*Photoset by Rowland Phototypesetting Ltd
Bury St Edmunds, Suffolk
Made and printed in Great Britain by
Richard Clay (The Chaucer Press) Ltd
Bungay, Suffolk*

CHAPTER ONE

CARLA Younger leaned back against the bar, surveying the throng about the gaming tables with that languid, rather bored expression which most of her friends would have recognised. Yet they would have been surprised to learn that her air of sophisticated ennui hid a nature that was shy and more than a little uncomfortable in the glamorous world she inhabited. How they would have laughed if they had known that Carla Younger, life and soul of all the wildest parties in the colony, didn't even care for the taste of alcohol. She had had lots of opportunities to convince herself otherwise and now took refuge in sipping any drink she was offered with painful slowness and even taking advantage of the nearest pot plant when that failed.

My God. Silently she reproached herself. What am I doing here? I'm supposed to be enjoying myself. I'm always pretending I'm doing that. Why? It was a question she found impossible to answer, but she continued to taunt herself with it. I don't care for drinking, I'm bored by gambling and Andy. Her eyes sought the fair curly head, located it at the centre table under the crystal chandelier where Andrew Ross was watching the wheel with rapt intensity, the chilling excitement so familiar among the casino regulars. It was as if their lives depended on the fickle irrationality of that tiny ball. Even Andy, who could stand there losing money from now till

Doomsday without feeling the pinch, even he would be feverish, elated if the ball fell right and he won a few dollars.

Her attention wandered, seeing without really registering the tatty seediness of the whole scene, the tables with the milling crowds, the pretty girl croupiers encouraging the faint-hearted, the haze of tobacco smoke hanging about the room, the dust-impregnated red velour of chairs and hangings. At least, impatiently she turned away, leaning with her elbows on the bar counter, if she did marry Andy—and who knows, with his persistence and her apathy they might just end up that way—she would know her father's money had no attraction for him. For even by Hong Kong's standards Andrew Ross was a very rich and an incredibly eligible young man. But it was her own motives which would be even more difficult to understand, for she didn't love him; couldn't imagine what life with him would be like. So what possible reason could she have for even contemplating the idea?

If she raised her head she could study herself in the smoky glass behind the bar. Beautiful, of course. It was something she had been told so often that now it meant scarcely anything to her, she could be perfectly dispassionate as she summed up what the mirror told her. Regular features apart from the too-wide mouth, eyes that had the greeny remoteness of deep water, emphasised by straight dark brows and smudged brown eyelids. Tonight the dull gold hair was swept back into a severe knot which drew attention to the long slender neck.

Still watching, she raised the glass to her lips, seeing the sparkle of expensive rings, the softer gleam of the heavy gold bracelet where the sleeve of her jacket fell back from her arm. Even her clothes, and that included this off-white trouser suit which she had bought with such single-minded extravagance on a visit to Paris last month, even they gave her little pleasure, the shopping sprees were mere habit.

Her father had, with his usual unerring accuracy, put his finger on it when he picked her up at the airport and had watched the pile of boxes with their Rome and Paris labels being carried to the car. His eyebrows had gone up in the quizzical arch which she knew was not intended as a criticism, although his words held a shade of censure.

'Do you think this is the answer, pet?'

'No, I suppose not.' She had shrugged, blushed a little and smiled, regretting the confidence which had led her to tell him that her trip overseas had been intended to relieve her boredom, now anxious only that her home-coming should not be marred by disagreement. 'Only in Paris a kind of madness overtakes the most sensible of women and,' she slipped a persuasive arm through his as they sat together in the air-conditioned coolness of the car, 'you know that lets me out, Daddy.'

Bob Younger's face had eased into a smile, although an almost imperceptible sigh escaped from his lips at the same time. 'I could argue about that.' But then they had gone on to talk about her trip to America and Europe.

Still, she dismissed recollection of that and turned again to her reflection. She did like this outfit, even if it didn't solve any basic problem. It was just right for the casual style of gaming here in Macao and its simple lines were redeemed by the softness of the silk blouse in a shade that almost matched her eyes.

So absorbed was she in her own melancholy thoughts that she failed to see in the dim reflection that Andrew had detached himself from the crowd and only when an arm crept round her waist did she realise that he was beside her. She turned, allowing her cheek to rest against his for a moment.

'So this is what you do when I'm not here.' His voice with its soft American accent was intimate and caressing, 'Toast your own reflection.'

Carla looked at him with an easing of tensions, a smile relaxing her features as the blue eyes admired her blatantly. 'I wasn't,' she denied, but without conviction.

'Oh I'm not blaming you, honey. Not at all. In fact I can't imagine anything I'd rather be doing.'

'Oh yes?'

'Sure.' He grinned disarmingly. 'That's what brought me over.' He rapped on the counter to attract the attention of the Chinese barman who was busy with some customers at the far end of the bar. Then when the man came up, 'Another bottle of the same, Lee.'

'Sure, Mr Ross.' He turned a tulip-shaped glass onto the counter and a moment later was easing out the golden-wrapped cork.

'Not for me.' Firmly Carla put down her glass on the far side of the bar. 'I don't want any more to drink.'

'Oh come on, honey. Have a heart. I thought we had come out to celebrate or something.'

'We are celebrating.' Carla was at her most intimidating when she was cool, firm and detached. 'All I'm saying is that I don't want any more to drink. I still haven't finished this.'

'Well, if I'd known,' Andrew sounded the faintest bit

sulky, 'I wouldn't have ordered another bottle. I don't want to have to drink the lot by myself.'

'Then don't.' Her answer was crisp. 'There's no reason why you should feel compelled to empty the bottle.'

'So be it.' Andrew decided that it was best to give in gracefully, 'But tell me, darling, what happened to you when you were in Europe? Did you run down a policeman when you had been drinking?'

'No.' There was a long silence. 'You should know that I never drink and drive. Nothing happened.' Deliberately she looked over his head and into the crowds.

'Sorry, Carla.' There was an uneasy look on Andrew's face which cleared when he finished the glass of champagne and turned to refill it. 'Why I really came over was to persuade you to come and try your luck. I've been losing steadily and I've a feeling that maybe you'll change it for me.'

'Not now, Andy.' Even as she spoke Carla knew that she was being unreasonable. After all, if she was going to be such a wet blanket she shouldn't have agreed to come gaming, they could have gone dancing instead. 'In a little while,' she softened. 'I'll just stay here for a bit so long as it's quiet. It won't be long before the crowds begin to flock in and it will be impossible to hang round the bar. You go back and I'll just sit here. I'll try to concentrate on your lucky numbers.'

'Bless you, honey.' Andy grinned at her, raised her hand to his mouth and then turned to resume his position at the tables, Carla's eyes following the one fair head among so many dark ones clustering round the table.

She wished she could respond to his suggestion with

more enthusiasm, as she would have done two years ago when she had first thrown herself into the giddy pleasure-seeking life of so many of her contemporaries in Hong Kong. What were you supposed to do if you were rich but enjoy yourself? She asked the question constantly, but in spite of that she was finding it difficult to enjoy life.

At one time she had, but it seemed a long time ago now. And she was unable to say whether the savour had gone suddenly, or whether it had simply ebbed away.

Impulsively she turned, rapping on the counter in a way that brought Lee hastily up from the other end. 'Yes, Miss Younger.' The sloe dark eyes were startled at this unusual sign of impatience from the cool English-woman.

She pushed her almost empty glass across to him. 'I don't want any more of this, Lee. But give me a tonic water with a dash of angosturas. And in the same kind of glass, please.'

'Ah.' The puzzled look cleared from his face as he turned to get what she had ordered and he smiled at her in understanding as he pushed the pale amber liquid across to her. 'Mr Ross think you are drinking champagne?'

'Exactly. And,' She put out a hand to the bottle which had been left close to her elbow, 'empty some of this out, Lee, just to make the whole thing more credible.'

'Empty?' The startled look was back, showing clearly that he could not see the sense of paying all those dollars for wines that were to be thrown out. Fortunately at that moment there was a sudden surge at the bar and demands for service diverted his attention.

Carla turned with a faint smile. What was the use? If Andy wanted to drink more than was good for him such a futile subterfuge wouldn't stop him. Not that he habitually drank a lot. But when he considered he had something to celebrate he could go over the top. Like tonight, their first meeting since she had come back from Europe, and his celebration had begun even before he picked her up by taxi from her home on the Peak.

She supposed, and her heart melted just a little when she caught sight of him as intent as ever on the roulette wheel, she ought to enter into the spirit of the thing and go and join him. A hand went out to raise the glass to her mouth and just then she felt the compulsive scrutiny of someone else's eyes. Her gaze flicked round the room from the crowds so busy about the tables and to the right of the main entrance.

Just inside the door, apparently part of a small group newly arrived, stood a man who was tall enough to look over the heads of his companions. And it was on Carla his eyes were fixed, giving the impression that he could have been watching her for some time. Even at that distance there was an intensity about him, a piercing strength about the cool gaze that was arresting.

All at once Carla was very conscious of the gold-topped bottle in the ice bucket at her elbow, the casual way she was apparently tossing liquor down her throat. The hand holding the glass trembled and she took it from her lips and set it down on the bar counter beside the bottle. Still he refused to release her from the power of his scrutiny, until at last one of his friends attracted his attention with a remark and Carla, with a shuddering little sigh, turned again to the bar.

She couldn't understand why she was disturbed. With an attempt at indifference she put up a hand to smooth her already immaculate hair. It was impossible to resist watching in the mirror just what was happening behind her and she was aware of a frisson of excitement as she saw the relaxed group of men walking over towards the bar, with the tall striking man towering over the others.

They congregated at the end farthest from her and she heard one of them order beers when Lee went forward to them. She sat staring ahead of her, for some reason anxious that no-one should suspect her of trying to attract attention to herself. This in itself was a novel experience, for Carla Younger had always forced herself to appear extrovert. But it was impossible to resist, under the pretext of taking a handkerchief from her handbag, a surreptitious glance along the counter.

At once she regretted it, for her eyes were immediately engaged by one of the group of newcomers who was looking at her with undisguised interest. But the man whom she had noticed had his back turned towards her with such firmness that she felt a blush begin to colour her cheeks.

It was a relief when Andy returned, as ebullient as he had been downcast a short time before and shaking his winnings in exaggerated triumph. 'Bless you, my sweet.' His voice was loud and carrying. 'I knew your faith would carry me through. You always bring me luck.' He bent his head and kissed the side of her neck.

At that moment, Carla glanced up and into the mirror, to see the man, no doubt attracted by Andy's penetrating voice, turn to look at them over his shoulder. Their eyes met briefly, then his flicked to Andy with a disparaging, slightly dismissive glance before he returned to his conversation with his friends.

For no reason Carla felt stung by what she decided was his patronising manner, which may have accounted for the eager way she responded to Andy. She slid off her stool with a smile that was quite dazzling.

'I'm glad, darling.' Her voice was deliberately drawling and affected. 'Now let's go and find somewhere to dance. It's such ages since we did that.' And with her head high, Andy trailing behind with a bemused expression on his face, she strolled to the door.

But while they danced at the large hotel further along the waterfront Carla felt even more disenchanted with herself. What on earth was the matter with her? Imagining that a total stranger had looked at her with disapproval. And even if he had, did it matter? Why should she worry about it? Surely she was old enough to know that it was what you felt about yourself, knew about yourself deep down that was important. But that too was a painful idea, one to be thrust aside.

Dully she moved round the room, trying to follow Andy's rather eccentric steps which were always half a beat behind the music. The months since they had last danced had encouraged her to forget that as far as rhythm was concerned, Andy had been missed out by the fairy who looked after such matters. And the one and a half bottles of champagne plus his earlier drinks had improved nothing. It had simply increased his confidence and determination so that now he was humming in her ear, introducing another distraction.

Carla sighed mournfully as they left the floor, going back to one of the tables arranged round the small dancing area. Andy would think it strange if she suggested they return to Hong Kong already, but that was what she wanted to do. She felt exhausted with her day of doing nothing and longed to be in her own bed at home.

'But honey . . .' Andy was less than willing. 'We've just come. You said come across to the gaming and then you refuse to play. Then you said dance and now you want to go home.' He frowned moodily. 'You're being very hard to please. And our first night too.'

'Yes, I know, Andy.' She made a determined effort not to snap. 'I'm feeling restless tonight. I just don't know what I want.'

'Don't you, honey?' At once a hand came out to cover hers as it lay listlessly on the table. 'I know what I want. What I've wanted for the last two years.'

'Oh, Andy. This isn't the time, or the place to talk about that.' She pulled her hand away and pushed back her chair. 'We have just over an hour before the last ferry. Let's go for a walk. It's a beautiful night.'

'A walk?' The consternation in her companion's voice made the girl smile.

'Yes, a walk. It's what people do with their legs, you know. Oh, I don't mean a route march. I simply mean what Daddy would call a "daunder along the front".' She laughed as she imitated her father's slight Scottish accent.

'Okay, okay. A daunder it shall be. Just remember I'm not used to walking.'

Outside the huge hotel, the air was soft and balmy after the coolness of the air-conditioned room they had left. Carla slipped her hand in Andy's arm as they turned to walk along the waterfront, quiet now except for the insistent lapping of the water.

This, she realised with a great wave of misplaced longing, was what she missed when she was in Europe. This soft heady atmosphere that was the essence of the mysterious land that was China. Even living on the fringe of that vast country as they did in Hong Kong, as they did here across the Pearl River in Macao, there was no escaping its influence.

It was in the air they breathed, in that evocative scent of fish and seaweed and incense, of camphor-wood and smouldering charcoal. It was in every aspect of life, from the teeming vital high-rise flats of Kowloon to the hard labouring life of the peasants in the New Territories as they planted their rice seedlings in the paddy fields. But at this moment it was standing here on the front at Macao, in the sparkle of the moonlight on the water, in the gentle rise and fall of the junks in the harbour.

Carla sighed and leaned for a moment against Andy's supporting arm.

'You sound unhappy, my sweet.' Encouraged by her softer manner he turned his head so that his mouth rested on her hair. 'In fact, it strikes me that you've been a bit out of sorts all evening. What's the matter?'

'Oh, nothing. Just a little sense of dissatisfaction with life in general and myself in particular.'

'Oh . . .' He laughed encouragingly. 'Why should you feel dissatisfied? Most people I know would be happy enough to change places with you.'

'I don't doubt it.' She spoke with a return of her old sharpness. 'But I doubt if they would be happy when they had changed.'

'Ouch.' He grimaced. 'You are prickly this evening.'

'Sorry.' It was a reluctant smile as they turned away from the waterfront, their steps leading aimlessly towards one of the narrow alleys leading through one of the old quarters of the town.

Carla could hardly have explained, even to herself, why the mood of mournful nostalgia should affect her so strongly that night. She had been to Macao dozens of times in recent years without being particularly affected, but this visit seemed tied in some mysterious way with those others when she had been a schoolgirl. When her mother had been alive.

How different life would have been if only . . . They had both missed her so bitterly. Her father and herself. But neither had been able to comfort the other. Perhaps they were too much alike. He with his rather Calvinistic restraint, his reluctance to show the depth of his feelings; and Carla at a particularly vulnerable age, following the lead he set. It had taken her mother with her outgoing, irrepressible attitudes to thaw the slightly shy, not quite taciturn Scotsman, to provide the link between him and his sensitive daughter.

She had been at school in Switzerland when she had first learned of her mother's illness. It had been a worry, but because the seriousness of it had been kept from her, the shock had been more severe when a 'phone call from her father had summoned her hurriedly back home ten days before the end of term in Lausanne.

The sight of her mother lying in the narrow hospital bed, looking so incongruous in one of the luxurious bedrooms, had been a shattering experience for the girl who had led such a protected life, who hadn't until then had the slightest idea of what real sorrow was. Gone was the pretty sun-tanned laughing face, in its place the pain-worn features of a dying woman, the pallid skin, the hair streaked with grey telling their own story.

Her mother had tried to smile, a smile that was torture to see, and had reached out a thin eager hand to take her daughter's.

'Darling.' Her voice was a mere thread. 'I'm so angry with Daddy making all this fuss. To call you back when you would have been home in just over a week in any case. Now you'll have missed all the end of term parties.'

'No. I shan't.' Afterwards, Carla could never understand how she kept back the tears that were bursting in her chest. In spite of her father's warnings when she had reached the house, she had been unprepared for this total change in her mother. 'We've had all the parties. So I was ready to come home.' She smiled down at the tired face looking at her with weary, drugged eyes, squeezed the limp hand which she held so tenderly in her own. 'I'm annoyed that Daddy didn't let me know sooner.'

'Oh, I wouldn't let him.' The girl had to bend down to catch the words. 'Such a fuss.'

Then the American nurse, with her white overall and her large white shoes, had come across the thick Chinese carpet. 'I think you'd better go now, Miss Younger. We don't want to tire the patient, do we?'

And Carla, reaching the door of the bedroom, had rushed past her father who was standing so helplessly on the landing outside and into her own room where she had thrown herself weeping onto the bed. She had been aware that her father had followed her, although it was a moment before he had spoken.

'You're best to cry, Carla.' His own voice was thick with anguish. 'It's the only thing to do.' His hand came down stroking her hair until she became quieter and turned round so that she was lying on her side and could see him on the chair drawn up to the bed.

'Why didn't you tell me? Why . . . ?' She tried to choke back the tears.

'She didn't want me to. It's only six weeks since she first went to see the doctor. He called me next day and told me that it was hopeless. Your mother insisted that you weren't to be brought home. She said that she would rather wait until you came back at the end of term in the usual way. But . . . when John Crawford saw her on Monday, he told me that he didn't think she would last.' He put a hand to his cheek and for the first time Carla noticed how ill he looked himself.

'Does Mummy know?'

'She knows that there's no hope. She insisted on being told the truth. She's been very brave, really. Only I haven't told her how imminent it is. She thinks I just decided to bring you home a bit earlier, that's all. I suppose the drugs dull the understanding.'

Carla took his hand and held it against her cheek, unable to reply at once. Then he spoke again.

'Don't speak about it to her, Carla. We've made all the arrangements together. She won't want you to be involved. Perhaps I was wrong to bring you home.' For the first time in her life he seemed to have lost his absolute certainty. 'It might have been better for you to avoid this . . .'

'No.' The denial was fierce and positive. 'No.' She began to weep again. 'No, Daddy. I want to be here.

With Mummy and with you.'

But although her intention to be close to her father, to try to comfort him, to be comforted by him, had been in her thoughts in those last days of her mother's life, somehow it hadn't worked out quite like that. The fact of the death, the gap it left in the household, seemed to have driven a wedge between them. The truth was that each was so anxious to avoid giving pain to the other that they scarcely spoke of the woman they were both mourning. In the succeeding years, after Carla returned from her spell in Scotland, when they were able once again to speak of happier times, they had become adept at avoiding mention of what had been so harrowing for them both.

Mr Younger threw himself into his business which meant that the pharmaceutical firm of which he was head went from strength to strength. And now he was listed as one of the wealthiest men in the Far East. Yet his daughter knew well enough that he was a disappointed man. It was more difficult for her to face up to the knowledge that she, his only child, was the source of that disappointment. A frivolous butterfly was not the kind of daughter for a man like Bob Younger.

Carla brought herself back to the present with a sigh and swallowed the lump caused by so much reminiscing.

'Let's take a look up here, Andy.' Her voice was falsely excited as she tried to drive away the threatening tears. 'It's years since I've been along these alleys and it used to be such a favourite place when I was at school. Did I tell you that once I wanted to be an architect?'

'I just don't believe it. Besides,' he went on after a moment's consideration, 'didn't you tell me at one time

you were going to be a nurse?' He laughed. 'Equally
unlikely I should say.'

'That was later.' Her voice was sharp. 'Much later.'

'So what? Maybe you wanted to be an airline pilot too.
I wanted to be a gambler on the Mississippi.'

She didn't reply but tried to regain her pleasure in the
charmingly old-fashioned wrought iron balconies with
flowers frothing over them. Only, Andy's words were
another reminder, however unconsciously spoken. A
reminder of the worthwhile career she might have had.
If she had had the staying power. But what the Dickens.
She hadn't, and that was the end of it. She had never
been cut out for a nurse. If she had been, she would have
found the strength to go on.

It was almost as clear as day with the moonlight
skimming between high chimneys and peeping over
crumbling walls which enclosed the sweet-scented gar-
dens. At each turn it seemed some memory returned to
haunt, time was almost forgotten as they turned a corner
and found themselves confronted by the towering façade
of a church.

'I didn't expect that.' She laughed in genuine pleasure. 'I had forgotten how close we were. Sao Paulo.'
She dredged her mind for the details she had once
known. 'Built by the Japanese in the 17th century.' With
a tiny questioning frown she turned to her companion.
'Can that be right do you suppose, Andy? Why the
Japanese?'

'Don't ask me, sweetie.' He shrugged and yawned,
not caring to hide his boredom. 'Seems most unlikely if
you really want my opinion.'

'It does. It does seem unlikely. Yet I'm convinced

that's what happened.' Her voice was more determined and cheerful than it had been earlier. 'What time is it?' It was difficult to read the figures on her tiny gold watch even though she held her wrist up to the light. 'Andy. We've got about ten minutes to catch the hydrofoil.' Dismay was in her eyes as well as her voice. 'Why didn't you tell me?'

'I forgot.' Andy was unconvincing. 'I didn't realise how far we had come.'

'I'm afraid I don't believe you.' Carla could be very chilly when she wanted. 'It seems to me we've been in this situation before.' She was referring to a time, earlier in their acquaintance, when Andy had taken her to one of the secluded beaches on the island for a moonlight swim and had arranged that his car should give trouble when it was time for them to return. The trouble had swiftly resolved itself when Carla had positively told him that she would walk to the nearest telephone and ask the chauffeur to come and collect them.

'You've been watching too many B movies,' she had accused drily as the engine roared into life after he 'found' a broken wire. 'If you have any plans for seduction, I would be glad if you would tell me beforehand. Then I could come prepared with a nightdress and a toothbrush.'

'I'll remember.' He had laughed rather sheepishly and thereafter had behaved fairly well, although soon he had begun to press her to marry him. So far she had resisted although she couldn't really say why. She had had lots of other men friends in the time she had known him. Some of them she had found intriguing and attractive, for a little while. But she always seemed to come back to

Andy. And she missed him when he was away.

They didn't speak to each other as they hurried, rather hopelessly, back to the harbour. In her heart Carla knew that it was her own fault just as much as his. She was the one most anxious to be home, she ought to have paid more attention to the distance they had wandered. Now, she would have to ring her father and tell him that she wouldn't be home after all. She knew, or rather she suspected, that he had some reservations about her friendship with Andy and she was careful to give him no grounds for thinking that their relationship was more intense than it was.

There had been no real hope of catching the ferry, nevertheless she felt an additional pang of annoyance when their expectations were confirmed on reaching the quay.

'Damn.' Breathless from rushing she faced him with eyes flashing. 'Damn. Damn. Why didn't you make sure we were back in time, Andy?' she asked unreasonably.

'Never mind, sweet.' He put an arm round her waist, smiling disarmingly into her disappointed face. 'We'll get a bed for the night at the Lisboa. And if it will make things easier for you I'll ring your father myself.'

'No, I prefer to do that,' she said a bit ungraciously. 'I don't want him to suspect the worst. Oh, and two beds if you don't mind. And two rooms.' She twisted from his grasp.

'Of course.' In spite of his ready agreement he sounded sulky, 'This is not a night I'd choose to share a bed with you, my dear. While you're in this disapproving mood I should be put off. Quite definitely.'

'You idiot.' In spite of herself Carla laughed, then

regretted it when his arm snaked about her waist again.

'I don't see why you have to check in with your father, Carla. You're old enough and shouldn't have to ask if you can stay out.'

'It's how I like it, Andy.' They had had the same argument before many times and she had no inclination to embark on it yet again.

'Still,' he grumbled on, 'most girls have their own flats these days. You'd think your father would realise. You're a big girl now, able to look after yourself.'

'Let's go along to the hotel, Andy.' Even if she had explained her reluctance to leave her father on his own she suspected Andy would not have understood. 'It's a nuisance we've missed the last hydro, but maybe it was my fault as much as yours.'

'It was, my sweet.'

There was no trouble about rooms and they were given two on the first floor, each with its own bathroom and opposite each other on the long corridor. When Carla closed the door of her small suite she leaned against it for a moment with a sigh of relief. All she wanted now was to have a quick shower, put a call through to her father and turn out the light. She pulled off her jacket and tossed it onto the wide double bed, then there was a quick tap at the door.

Damn you, Andy, she thought as she went over and threw it open. 'What on earth . . .' She found a glass of whisky pushed into her hands and Andy raising another to his lips in a mocking salute.

'To you, my darling. To your sparkling eyes.' He stepped towards her, but before he could put his foot over the threshold, Carla with considerable presence of mind, slid past him so that he had no choice but to join her in the corridor.

'Andy,' she sighed with resignation. 'What on earth do you want? You know I don't drink whisky.' She folded her arms, still holding the glass against the green silk of her blouse.

'I wanted,' Andy struggled to collect his thoughts, 'I wanted to see you, my love. All the time you've been away I've been longing to see you.' Mournfully he tried to focus his eyes on her. 'Longing,' he repeated.

'That's all right.' She struggled to hang onto her patience. 'Now you have, Andy, dear. Goodnight.' She pressed a swift kiss on his cheek and moved towards her open door.

'No, Carla.' Perhaps encouraged by her mildness, Andy grabbed her, pulling her into his arms, ignoring the whisky which spilled down her front, oblivious of two glasses rolling over the deeply carpeted floor. 'I want you, darling. Tonight.' He would have been masterful if his words had been less slurred.

Suddenly Carla had had enough. This was not her idea of a night out, not struggling with a man who had had too much to drink, not being deprived of a night's sleep in her own bed. 'Andy!' He was holding her so tightly that she could hardly breathe and her attempts to free herself were fruitless.

She wasn't even aware of the arrival of the lift till she caught sight of several figures advancing along the corridor towards them. 'Andy!' Scarlet with embarrassment she hissed warningly in his ear, but that seemed only to inflame his determination.

'Be good, sweetheart!' The words were loud and only

slightly blurred, 'you said you wanted to get to bed. And so do I.' As he swung her round and in through the door of her suite, Carla took in the amused glances from the group of men whom she had seen downstairs in the bar. And impassive, but nevertheless conveying a strong impression of disapproval, was the tall dark man whom she had noticed so forcefully. The door clicked behind them and she was alone with Andy. Looking into his silly face and very much aware that they both stank of whisky Carla felt totally humiliated and stepped quickly away when his arms slackened.

'Now,' she hissed angrily, 'Now *you* can go back to bed in your own room.'

'Okay.' He grinned and stepped unsteadily forward. 'Okay, honey.' He opened the door with a slight flourish. 'I just thought it was worth a try.'

When the door had closed again behind him Carla stared at the panel of smooth mahogany, making a deliberate effort to control the impulse to burst into emotional tears. She couldn't begin to understand what was the matter with her. Tonight seemed to have been doomed from the start, when she had opened the door to Andy smelling slightly of gin and tonic, by her inability to throw off her boredom at the casino and most of all by the nostalgia when she had wandered through the narrow streets of Macao.

She had a childish longing to call her mother's name, to feel the warmth of the comforting arms about her, to be soothed as she had been when she had been a girl. Somehow all the dissatisfaction she felt, in her life, in herself, were crystallised in what had happened after her mother's death, in the emotional way she had rushed off to begin nursing. And in the way she had given it up, equally in a wave of emotional despair.

She hadn't confessed to anyone the whole truth of that unhappy episode. Unhappy—how inadequate the word was for an experience that had torn her to pieces. She had just been picking herself up after eighteen months, a year and a half when she had thrown herself into her work, sparing herself nothing on the wards and studying most of the nights. It was then, just at the right time, that Hamish Davidson had come along to sweep her off her feet.

He had been a giant of a man, physically and emotionally, a surgeon who had the time to sit with his patients, to explain exactly what he intended doing, to reassure, to give them confidence.

That was what he had done for Carla. He had noticed her on the wards, seemed to sense her loneliness, then taken her under his wing, drawing her out, forcing her to speak about her mother till much of the pain was eased away. He made her take up climbing with him, watched with satisfaction while she blossomed and relaxed in the happy-go-lucky group with whom he spent his spare time.

In no time at all she was madly in love with him. Even when she was busy she could sense when he appeared in the ward and always his eyes sought her out, he would flick a special look in her direction when he was deep in conversation with Sister Muirie and she would know that he was telling her that he would see her that night. And his love-making, a mixture of tenderness, gentleness and passion, told her that his feelings were very similar to her own.

She couldn't take it when he died. With the same terrible suddenness and from the same disease that had killed her mother. God knows *that* had been bad enough, but he had forced her to accept it. And now at thirty, he had gone. It was too much for her to bear. She packed her things and left Edinburgh just two weeks before she would have taken her final exams. He had been meaning to take her out to a special restaurant to celebrate. But without him life had lost all its savour. There was no purpose in it, no point in pretending she was cut out for nursing. She couldn't stand the thought of it any more.

'You haven't forgotten about tomorrow night, Carla?' Mr Younger folded his copy of the *Wall Street Journal* and handed his empty cup across the breakfast table for refilling.

'No, of course not, Daddy.' With deft fingers she raised the china pot then handed back the coffee with a smile. 'Do I ever fail to exert my charm on your dull millionaires?'

'No.' His mouth moved in a slightly reluctant smile. 'I must confess that you don't. Even though you must find it boring at times, you never let it show.'

'Of course I don't find it boring.' She was anxious to coax him from the disapproval which had affected him since her return the previous morning from Macao. 'I'm glad you bring your friends home rather than take them out to eat . . . It's good for me to have something to do other than enjoy myself.' She would have hated him to know just how little she seemed able to do that. 'Besides,' impulsively she rose and walking behind him laid her cheek briefly against his thick grey hair, 'I like doing things for you, in case you hadn't noticed.'

'Do you?' The genuine surprise in his voice was hardly complimentary she thought wryly, but she could see that he was touched. Then rather gruffly as she straightened up and walked over to the window, 'Are you asking young Ross?'

'Andy?' She relaxed against the window frame, looking down at the busy waterway that lay at the foot of the Peak. 'I hadn't thought about it. I still don't feel very pleased with him for letting me miss the ferry the other night. Perhaps a little neglect would make him pay more attention to the time after this. But maybe I'd better not make too much of it. After all, I had mentioned the party to him so maybe I'll forgive him. Do you mind?'

'Of course not. You know that I've never interfered with your choice of friends.'

'Oh, Daddy.' She laughed without meaning to. 'That's not very enthusiastic about poor Andy. He's easy-going and good-natured, you know.'

'I know all about his good qualities.' He rustled his paper again. 'He's a nice enough lad. Just not quite the man I'd like to see you settle down with.'

'And who do you have in mind? I should have thought that Andy would have been most people's idea of the ideal son-in-law.'

'Ah, but I'm not most people.' He rose and walked over to join his daughter by the window. 'And luckily, we're in the position where money doesn't matter. A rich husband isn't necessarily the right one for you.'

'And a poor one? I seem to remember a little resistance to a certain Jamie Conroy.'

'Oh, he was a mere fortune-hunter.'

Carla sighed. 'Parents can be very hard to please. But you ought to have known that I wasn't interested in Jamie.'

'I did know.' The smile faded slowly from his face, revealing his more normal reserved expression. 'For you only the best kind of marriage is good enough.' He paused. 'Like the one your mother and I had.'

Surprised by his reference to her mother, Carla put a finger to her lips and bit it hard. 'Isn't that strange,' her voice was low, 'when we were in Macao, I took Andy for a walk round the old town. It was filled with memories. So really,' her voice wasn't quite steady, 'it was my fault that we missed the boat. Just as much as poor Andy's.'

It was a long time before he answered and she knew that he too was remembering. But when he did speak, he was as matter-of-fact as ever. 'Of course you must ask him. But now,' He glanced at his watch, 'I must go. Khim will be waiting. I'll leave it to you to decide what kind of meal, Carla. You know the kind of thing. Oh, and wear one of your pretty new dresses. As I've just seen the bills for some of them I might as well try to get some positive benefit.'

'I will.' Encouraged by the unexpected rapport that seemed to have developed between them, she slipped her hand through his arm and walked with him, through the spacious hall and out onto the drive where the Rolls stood, the grey-liveried chauffeur flicking its impeccable surface with a feather-duster. 'Good morning, Khim.'

'Good morning, Miss Carla.'

She leaned on the open sill when her father wound down the window. 'I have just the sort of dress that will do your tired business friends a power of good.'

'Nothing too extreme, pet.' For a moment Mr Younger looked anxious.

'Of course not, Daddy darling.' She blew a casual kiss as the car slid away from the front door. 'It will be just right.'

And it was, she decided the following evening as she looked at her reflection in the mirror, it was absolutely, stunningly, all right. Peony pink, the vendeuse had assured her when she bought it that day in Paris. A pale warm shade that emphasised the satiny tan of her shoulders beneath the narrow straps. The handkerchief peaks of the hem swirled round her slim legs when she moved, floating almost, the material was so light and sheer. The whole beauty of the dress was concentrated in the silk and in the simple, perfect lines. The bodice was plain, cut straight across and not too daringly low. To relieve the simplicity she hung a silver chain round her neck with a dangling crystal pendant which matched her earrings and on her fingers was the usual assortment of rings.

Tonight her hair was in a softer fashion than usual, in what she called her cottage loaf style, bundled on the top with careful negligence like a little girl about to have a bath. Carla gave a little whirl of pleasure at the sight of herself and, delighted to discover that she had thrown off her black mood, walked over to the door of her room.

She had often thought that it was the perfect setting for a party. No matter how far she travelled, she had never found any view that quite came up to the one that she had known since childhood. The whole bay could be seen from the terrace where the guests were congregating, the strings of lights along the decks of liners as they passed into and out of the harbour and further away, all the dazzling busyness of the Kowloon side.

Carla was enjoying herself as she flitted back and forward among the guests, most of whom she had known all her life. One or two were strangers to her, but she had always been at ease in company and she was good at making visitors feel welcome. Her father was moving round having a word with his colleagues, flirting just a little with the wives but always retaining that slight aloofness that was probably necessary for the chairman of the company.

He stopped Carla when she was leaving one group of acquaintances and moving on to the next. 'No sign of your young man yet?'

'I think I hear him now.' She wrinkled her nose at her father and moved through the terrace doors into the sitting-room which was softly lighted by beautiful lamps, with hand-painted china bases and pink silk shades.

Above the chatter of the guests, she had heard the crunch of car tyres and, as she expected, the door opened and Jenny showed the new arrival into the room. But the man with her certainly was not Andy. He was dark and much taller than the man she had been expecting.

Carla stopped abruptly, the smile on her lips faded and the hand she had been holding out dropped as she looked up into the dark, rather austere eyes. She had thought when she encountered him in the corridor in the hotel the other night that he had a withdrawn and rather self-contained look. But now, and it gave her a little twitch of pleasure, she saw that he was as surprised at the unexpected meeting as she was herself. Obviously he was one of her father's guests, he had mentioned a Doctor something-or-other whom he was expecting.

She was about to hold out her hand again and introduce herself when Mr Younger stepped into the room with an enthusiatic greeting.

'Ah, Marc, my dear boy. I was beginning to wonder what had happened to you. No problems finding your way, I hope?'

'No. Thank you, sir.' The smile he turned on his host was, Carla decided, rather nice and even hinted that he might be slightly shy. And his accent, certainly not speaking English as a native, was more than a little intriguing. 'No trouble. Only I was rather later than I had intended getting through with the committee I mentioned to you.'

'That doesn't matter so long as you're here. I hope everything went well for you. No problems. Now let me introduce you to my daughter, Carla.' He put an arm round the girl's shoulders. 'This my dear, is Dr Marc Gérard. He's doing some work for the WHO at the moment. But I'm glad that he's been able to tear himself away from his patients for a few days.'

Carla felt strange when her outstretched hand was taken in his firm cool grip, he murmured something and made a slight formal bow.

'You are fortunate, sir, to have such a beautiful daughter. Her husband must consider himself extremely lucky.'

Mr Younger laughed and gave Carla an affectionate squeeze. 'You are away ahead of me, Marc. So far as I know there's no sign of her finding a husband.'

Just then the door opened again and another pair of guests was shown into the room. With a murmur of apology Mr Younger went forward to greet them without appearing to notice the sudden tension between his daughter and the doctor. They stood staring at each other for a moment, Carla with her cheeks blazing as she considered the only construction it was possible for him to put on that last encounter in the hotel corridor. She knew she was not imagining the coolness she read in his expression.

'Miss Younger.' It seemed an age before he broke the silence. 'I beg your pardon.' There was no need for him to explain what he meant so she chose to ignore the matter.

'Dr Gérard. How very kind of you to come and see us.' Insincerity sounded in her voice. She began to lead him towards the terrace, holding up a hand for one of the maids to come over with her tray of drinks. 'Am I right in thinking that you are to be on the island for just a few days.'

'Yes, that is so. Just as soon as possible I have to get back to my patients.'

'Oh come now!' She smiled as she raised her glass to her lips. 'Surely even a busy doctor is entitled to a holiday.'

He was silent for so long that she thought he hadn't heard, but just as she was about to make some other inconsequential remark, he spoke. 'The trouble is, Miss Younger,' his tone was quite mild, 'when I am not there my patients simply die. There is no-one else who can do my work. You see, I am working among the natives of

Dalaoa Island, one of the North Gauran group.' He paused, and his eyes moved slowly over her face and figure. 'I suspect, Miss Younger, that you spent more on the dress you're wearing than the whole of the population of Dalaoa spends on food in a year.'

CHAPTER TWO

As anger rose in Carla, the colour drained from her face,
she felt herself tremble with rage. They stared at each
other, she searching her mind for some retort that would
at least put him in his place. It would be impossible to
find words that would knock him from the pedestal
which he had put himself on, it would take some more
skilful rhetoric than she herself possessed to do that. But
it would be pleasant to let him know that civilised
people, no matter what their private opinions, did not,
at a first meeting, take the opportunity to be offensive to
their hostess. The silence between them lengthened, she
felt her breast heaving with the strength of her feelings
and was about to open her mouth to lash him with an icy
comment when an arm slid round her waist and an
intimate voice murmured in her ear.

'Darling, I'm so sorry I'm late.'

Carla looked round at Andy's apologetic smiling face,
but she paid scant attention and turned to deliver her
coup de grâce. Only by then all she could see of the
doctor was his retreating back as he strolled away from
them, to be greeted with enthusiasm by the glamorous
French wife of one of the company's chief chemists.

The encounter had the effect of making Carla, going
among the guests with her head held high, still smarting
with indignation against Marc Gérard, exert herself to
be the perfect hostess. During the remainder of the

evening she avoided his eyes, but she was never free from the baleful influence of his presence. She wouldn't admit, even to herself, that no-one else seemed to share her opinion of him, in fact he seemed to be the man who was sought out by men and women alike and was the centre of a laughing chattering group each time she caught sight of his tall figure.

During the buffet meal produced with the impeccable unobtrusiveness which Jenny always managed, Carla sat on one of the brocade window seats, talking to John Herbert who was her godfather as well as one of the family's best friends. She pushed the delicious mixture of crab quick-fried with egg sauce, served with rice and vegetables round her plate, trying to disguise from herself and her companion that she had completely lost her appetite. But after a moment, John, with a glance at her from beneath his beetling brows, smiled.

'What's this, Carla? Aren't you eating? Don't tell me that you're on diet like the rest of your sex.'

'No, of course not, Uncle John. I had a bigger lunch than usual, that's all,' she lied.

'Well, it's as good as Jenny's cooking usually is. But if you're not hungry . . . I hope you aren't sickening for something. Or perhaps you're in love.' He looked round the room. 'Didn't I see Andy Ross a moment ago?'

'You're being very subtle.' Carla's laugh was rueful rather than amused. 'And yes you did see Andy. I just sent him over to have a word with Joan Christison. I thought she was looking a bit left out of things. Since James died, she seems rather to have dropped out of our circle.'

Carla wasn't looking at her godfather so she missed

the quick glance that he gave her before following the direction of her gaze through the glass and onto the terrace. 'Yes,' he agreed quietly. 'We haven't seen so much of her, but now I think she's beginning to pick up the threads again. It's time after two years . . .' He paused. 'I was speaking to Marc Gérard today in the office. An interesting, unusual young man I would say.'

'Interesting?' All the lack of concern she could muster was in her voice, but she held her breath while she waited for him to continue.

'Yes. It seems he's interested in some of our new products.'

'Does that make him interesting? Or unusual?' She teased.

'Well no. Not in itself,' he laughed. 'But you know me, Carla. I don't know much about the pharmaceutical side, I'm just the company secretary after all. I leave the glamorous side to the boys in the labs. No, I didn't mean that. What I meant was that I heard that he had rather a reputation in the field of genetics. Then he gave it up to take up this job with the WHO. Now he's on some tiny island in the back of beyond dealing with some very primitive tribes. From what I hear he's having to cope with not only the medical side but trying to convince them that the wheel is something that they've all been waiting for.'

'Oh, surely not.' Through the window she could see the subject of their discussion speaking and laughing with Hélène Veyriet, who was looking like the cat who had just swallowed the cream. 'There aren't places like that any more.'

'Well, perhaps I'm exaggerating. But it strikes me that

it takes rather an exceptional man to throw up all the comfort of a university appointment to do a job like that. Maybe,' and he turned an amused face to her so that she knew he had no intention of being taken seriously, 'maybe he's running away from an unhappy love affair.'

'I should think that highly unlikely.' She spoke as lightly as her companion. 'Dr Gérard doesn't look like the kind of man to let any woman upset him very much. And,' her eyes lingered on Hélène's animated face, 'I'm sure he will always find it easy to bring them to heel.' There was a shade of waspishness in her voice that made her companion look at her in surprise.

In view of her feelings for the doctor it was something of an embarrassment to find herself sitting opposite him the next day, eating lunch in the dining-room overlooking the bay. It was Saturday, when her father usually lunched at home and the one day that Carla, provided she wasn't abroad, kept free for him. She had been slightly annoyed when he had rung about twelve to say that he would be bringing someone with him for lunch. After last night's party she had been looking forward to a relaxed easy meal on the terrace, but that arrangement had had to be changed when Jenny had relayed the message which had arrived when Carla was wandering about in the garden picking some fresh flowers.

Then when the visitor turned out to be Marc Gérard, she wondered if her manner had shown even momentary disapproval. Something about the rather sardonic expression when he replied to her greeting told her that her attempts to disguise her feelings had been less than successful. However, as the meal progressed she had to admit that he could, when it suited him, be an amusing, interesting conversationalist. For once, Carla adopted the rôle of listener, a rôle that was partly forced on her because the men were discussing business to a large extent, but one which suited her since she hadn't forgiven their guest for his rudeness the previous night. Besides, she was glad to have the opportunity to study him without his being aware of the fact.

During the night when she had slept badly she had come to the conclusion that her first estimation of his looks had been misguided. She had decided that there was a mean twist to his lips, a cold unfeeling expression in the dark grey eyes. But now, talking animatedly to her father, none of these qualities showed, his mouth actually smiled with genuine amusement revealing startlingly white teeth and he sometimes ran a hand through the thick dark hair in a way that was youthful and disarming.

Not that she was disarmed. Not in the least. Only, she was just enough to admit to herself, if they had met in different circumstances, if he hadn't been so infernally rude . . . She realised that the men had stopped talking and that she herself was the subject of intense scrutiny from across the table. Colour rose in her cheeks and in an attempt at assurance she turned to her father with a tiny air of enquiry.

'Sorry, Daddy. I was miles away.' She smiled. 'I thought you were talking drugs.' Although she was no longer looking at him, she sensed that Marc Gérard's expression had changed now that he was being forced to look at the daughter of the house.

'I was saying, Carla, that I shan't be at home tonight. I was asking what you would be doing.'

'You won't be at home?' Dismay and, to her annoyance, a note of peevishness sounded in her voice. She stared at her father, surprised that he was fidgetting with his fork, not looking at her. 'But . . .' She was about to ask why but something held her back. She smiled, surprised how difficult it was to act naturally with that disapproving presence opposite. 'Well, it doesn't matter. I'll probably just read. I bought a book when I was in London and I haven't had the chance to start on it yet.'

'Oh you can read any time.' Her father's voice had a trace of something she couldn't quite identify. Almost as if he had been dreading her reaction to his statement. 'Why don't you do something with Marc. I know that he's going to be at a loose end till he flies off tomorrow.' His eyes moved guiltily from his daughter to his guest.

'Oh I don't think . . .'

'Oh I don't think . . .'

Both spoke at the same time and then stopped abruptly. With a smile and heightened colour Carla turned to her father. 'There you are, Daddy. I'm sure Dr Gérard could think of a dozen things he would rather do . . .'

'Don't be silly, Carla.' There was an impatience in Mr Younger's manner which surprised his daughter into speechlessness. 'And why don't you call him Marc? I thought it was my generation that was the formal one. I'm sure he'd be only too pleased.'

'Of course.' The doctor's interruption was smooth while the cool grey eyes continued to mock her. 'I was going to say that I was sure Miss Younger, Carla,' he smiled briefly, apologetically at his host, 'would have much more to do than take pity on a tourist trying to fill in the last few hours of his stay in Hong Kong.'

'Not at all.' Her voice was cool and clipped. 'I shall be pleased to show you round this evening. What would you like to do?'

'Now what would you be doing if I weren't here, Carla?'

'I . . .' She shrugged. 'I don't know.' Feverishly she searched her mind for the most innocuous way of passing the time. 'We could go to the cinema . . .'

'Oh no. Not the cinema.' Mr Younger spoke, interrupting without realising it the invisible combat between them. 'The weather's too beautiful to spend the evening indoors. If she were on her own, or with some of her friends, she would be off to the casinos in Macao. Or perhaps out to one of the beaches where they could swim.'

'Not the casinos.' His veto was firm, not troubling to make any enquiries about her own preferences. 'But a moonlight swim . . .' The dark eyes were speculative, assessing. '. . . That sounds a very attractive proposition.'

'Then . . .' Mr Younger took control of the arrangements with a disregard for his daughter's wishes that was unusual, '. . . Carla can pick you up from your hotel and drive you to wherever you decide to go.' He glanced at his daughter with raised eyebrows. 'Where do you think you'll make for? Shek O? Or Repulse Bay?'

'I haven't decided yet. Which do you think best, Daddy?' There was a shade of dryness in her voice. Then before he could answer she turned to their guest. 'Or perhaps we could leave the final decision to Marc.' Although she spoke sweetly she made certain that he would not mistake the veiled hostility in her manner.

'I shall be happy to leave it to you, Carla.' The look in his eyes was a direct contradiction of the mildness of his words. 'You know the colony so much better than I do. And perhaps we could go on somewhere afterwards where we can eat.'

Carla was still trying to decide how to respond to what she saw as the challenge in his eyes when her father spoke and pushed back his chair. 'Then that's settled,' he said with relief. 'I think we'll have coffee outside.'

It was just before seven when Carla drove her white MG sports car, twisting down from their home on the Peak, on to Lugard Road, then down towards the harbour area. She was excited, uptight, a result, so she told herself, of being forced into this meeting which she didn't want with a man she disliked. Whatever the cause, her emotions were reflected in her driving which showed a trace of recklessness although she was never in less than full control of the car.

When she pulled up with a screech of brakes outside the Mandarin Hotel on Connaught Road, she gave an involuntary little glance in the rear mirror, relieved that there was no sign of a police presence behind her. More than once she had been warned about her tendency to break the speed limit and only her conscious exertion of charm on the young men who had cautioned her had saved her from the penalties of the law.

She was about to swing her long legs out of the car when a figure she recognised came from the hotel towards her.

'Hello.' He tossed his small grip onto the back ledge, waited till she had resumed her seat before slamming the door and a moment later had slipped into the passenger seat beside her.

'Where are we heading for?' He didn't ask the question until they had rejoined the dense flow of traffic and she was less occupied with driving, but she had been annoyingly conscious of him, half-slewed round in his seat, making no attempt to hide the fact that he was studying her.

'Shek O, I thought. It will be less crowded there than Repulse.' Her reply was brief, hiding whatever emotion she was experiencing. And she was being confused and unnerved by trying to decide just what effect this man was having on her.

They left the built-up area behind them and went skimming along the narrow twisting roads with a speed that frightened and exhilarated. A devil seemed to have taken over and it gave her a grim sense of pleasure to see that his head had turned away from her and was looking at the road snaking about in the headlights, disappearing, being swallowed up underneath the bonnet. Once or twice she glanced at his feet on the thick pale carpeting and was disappointed not to see them thrust down nervously. She pressed her foot remorselessly onto the accelerator, feeling the smooth, almost imperceptible, increase of the power under her hands. Her head moved with a jerk when she realised that he was speaking to her. Inwardly she laughed. It was nice to think she had put the wind up him for he was asking her to slow down.

'Look.' A long brown finger pointed ahead to where they could just see a pull-in on the side of the road. 'Stop there for a moment, please.'

She hesitated. Then the idea flashed into her mind

that he might be one of those people who suffered from car-sickness. She swung the car from the road in a cloud of reddish dust and looked at him enquiringly. 'Well?' There was no friendliness in her voice. 'What's the matter?' She switched off the engine, trying to decide in the half-darkness whether he looked particularly pale.

'Nothing is the matter.' His voice was mildness itself. He rattled a bunch of keys in his hands. 'Except that I've decided to drive the car.'

Carla gave a gasp of anger when she realised he had taken the keys from the ignition. Then she gave a short little laugh. 'So . . .' she drawled. 'You *were* scared? I couldn't quite decide.'

'I didn't care for the way you were driving. No,' he admitted.

'It might interest you to know that I was Ladies Champion Driver for two years running. I am quite competent, you know.' Still she spoke in that condescending, amused voice.

'Oh, I don't doubt that. I can see that you know how to handle the machine. But unfortunately it takes more than that to make a good driver. It takes a little imagination and that, it seems, is something you don't have.' Without waiting for a reply he got out, came round to the driver's door and held it open for her. 'Now get out.' It was the tone of a man used to having his wishes obeyed and it stung the girl.

'And what if I don't? Do you mean to make me?' she jeered.

'If necessary.' In the light from the headlights the dark eyes glittered down at her with something like menace. 'But . . .' and now his voice had a suggestion of threat too '. . . it would be so much easier if you would just walk round and get into the passenger seat.'

For a moment she sat glaring up at him. It even occurred to her that she might snatch the keys dangling so temptingly from the fingers that held open the door. It gave her a brief feeling of triumph to imagine that she could slam the door, have the keys in the ignition in a flash and that he could be left in the middle of the road foolishly watching the rear lights disappearing.

But the pleasing dream of retaliation was short-lived, fading totally as she became aware of the impatience in his eyes. With an appearance of grace and a little laugh suggesting condescending amusement, she got out of the driving seat and went round to the passenger side, resisting the temptation to bang the door in temper.

'Thank you.' As he leaned forward to insert the key in the ignition, she surprised a gleam of amusement on his face. 'One thing I hate is rowing with a pretty woman.'

Trying to subdue the absurd spasm of pleasure that shot through her at his casual unexpected compliment, she wrenched her eyes from his and looked straight ahead of her.

'Drive on.' She had to struggle to overcome the inclination to laugh at the imperious sound of her instruction. 'I'll let you know when to turn off.' And her voice now had an almost humble note.

He was a good driver. However reluctant she was to admit it, she could only admire his competent handling of a strange car on dark roads that he did not know. And she quite enjoyed the sensation of being driven. Usually when they were out together, she drove Andy and her father too preferred not to drive now that he said the roads had become so impossible.

They crept forward into the almost empty parking place on the edge of the sand that was Shek O beach. Carla, who had always loved the spot, thought that she had never seen it lovelier and she got out of the car to stand gazing, all resentment of the tall figure who was so close beside her forgotten. On both sides of the swathe of pale sand, mountains swept down into the sea, cutting off the small bay from the rest of the island. From behind one of the sheer slopes the moon peeped coyly, white and cool and utterly enchanting, scattering the water with a million winking stars.

'It's quite a place.' His deep voice had taken on a less abrasive note, one that was warm and sensuous as if he were moved by the beauty of the perfect solitary moment as she was herself.

'Yes.' As she answered, she turned towards him, seeking in his expression an echo of her own bounding pulses. Their eyes met, intensely.

'Thank you for bringing me.' The unexpected warmth in his manner was too sudden for her to cope with.

'Feel free.' She gave an uncertain little laugh and ran away from him, up the beach in the direction of the changing rooms.

The sea was soft and warm as silk. They swam together, without speaking, to the furthest curve of the bay, then clambered out onto a small ledge where the dark sweep of the mountains could be seen extending to the next bay, and the next. Carla ignored his offered hand as she heaved herself from the water; she was too conscious of the impressive muscularity of his tall body to want to risk direct contact.

She had been unable to decide his reaction when she had come running down the beach to join him and even wondered with a touch of pique if he had one. She was used to her slender curvy form drawing admiring comments from her escorts and the one-piece bathing costume she was wearing enhanced, rather than concealed her attractions. She wouldn't admit that she had chosen the new swimsuit in black and white striped material which clung to her figure and left one silky shoulder bare, she wouldn't admit that she had decided to wear it simply to excite his interest. Why should she admit it when it wasn't true?

Without thinking about it any longer she dived straight into the deep dark water and began her powerful crawl back to the shore. Behind her, she felt the regular plash of his stroke, first at her heels then drawing level with her, but she showed no sign until she was wading through the shallows to the warm dry sand of the beach.

'The sea was lovely.' She spoke without thinking, similing up as if he had been Andy.

'Yes, I enjoyed it. But now I'm feeling hungry. Where shall we eat?'

'I'll meet you in fifteen minutes and we can decide.' Carla disappeared into the beach hut to have a shower under jets of warm fresh water, then to dry her hair in one of the coin-operated hair driers, brushing it till it hung in long smooth swathes.

When she was ready her final glance in the mirror had more than a trace of satisfaction. Tonight he couldn't accuse her of robbing the children of his precious island for the dress she was wearing was simple in the extreme. In fact she had chosen it with the hope that he would make just one crack. Then she could tell him, with tremendous relish, that she had bought the material, a cotton lawn in deep green covered with wild squiggles in navy, at one of the market stalls and that Jenny's sister had made it up for her. She ran a hand over her glossy shoulder-length hair and turned to the door.

'I think we should go and eat at Aberdeen.' She had allowed him to take the driving position without protest and now they were accelerating up the beach road. 'If you care for fish, that is.'

'Fine.' He seemed disinclined to talk and as there were lots of signs it was unnecessary for her to give any directions.

When they reached Aberdeen village Carla stood on the quayside watching while he backed the car into a vacant parking space, locked the door then came across to where she was waiting. Already, although she had given no sign, several sampans had edged out from their mooring spots manoeuvred around the flight of steps that led down to the water, while their owners tried to catch the eye of the young woman who was obviously intending to dine in one of the huge floating restaurants in the middle of the harbour.

The multi-decked craft still made Carla feel that they had escaped from some lavish American musical depicting life on the Mississippi steam boats at the turn of the century. They were bright with lights, coloured and hung about the decks in strings, serene and luxurious among the thousands of small craft crowding the natural harbour. Entire families, indeed generations lived out their lives on the sampans such as those who were plying for hire now, acting as ferries for the restaurants.

Laid out on the sides of the quay the day's catch was now being dried, thousands of fish netted during the morning had been gutted instantly and spread out on the ground where the effects of sun and air evaporated the moisture, enriching the evening with a characteristic scent. Children, dark slanting eyes bright with interest, caps of black hair painted on their skulls, crouched alongside ready with their sticks and short raucous cries to discourage idle marauding dogs who came too close. And if occasionally the attention of the small guards showed signs of wandering a peremptory word from one of the craft, in rows ten, twenty deep, soon restored their attention and reminded them that life was a serious business.

Carla turned her consideration to the hovering group of sampans, exchanged a few rapid words with the women operators and then, without consulting Marc, decided which boat would ferry them across the harbour. The women in the other craft leaned on their shoulder poles, moving silently, skilfully away while the selected boat was negotiated swiftly to the foot of the steps.

Soon they were sitting opposite each other in the most famous of the restaurants and Marc Gérard was frowning over the long menu which had been put into his hands.

'What would you like, Carla? Any preferences? Or taboos?'

She shrugged, resenting the fact that he hadn't looked at her when he spoke. 'I don't mind. I can eat most things. The only thing I never do when I'm here is go down and choose my meal from one of the tanks.' She shuddered, an affected little gesture calculated to gain his attention. To her surprise he laughed and put down the menu as if he had decided what they would eat. His gaze seemed to wander over her hair before returning to her face. 'Don't tell me you're squeamish. I can't believe that.'

'I don't see why you shouldn't.'

'You're right of course. And I rather agree with you.' He raised one dark eyebrow. 'Does that surprise you?' He smiled. 'Perhaps it does me. But anyway, I think it's a bit cold-blooded deciding which of the poor things has to be slaughtered for one's meal.' The approach of the waiter interrupted them and Carla listened while he ordered a meal she knew she would enjoy.

During the time they were eating she learned a lot about the man sitting opposite. Of course she had known that he was a German-speaking Swiss, that he had worked in Geneva until he had gone to his island two years earlier, but now he began to fill in all the intimate little details, about his brother who had just entered medical school, a brother who was nineteen and who had been born when he himself was fifteen. Carla's maths was equal to calculating that her escort was thirty-four.

'But now,' he smiled and offered the dish of hors d'oeuvres, 'I've been talking too much, tell me about yourself.'

'There's nothing much to tell about me.' As she nibbled a piece of pickled cucumber Carla experienced the now familiar feeling that she was well on the path to a wasted life. She shrugged in an effort to be casual. 'I travel a lot.' Compared with his usefulness it was woefully inadequate and the dark eyes looking at her with the habitual intentness appeared to confirm the low opinion she held of herself. It was on the tip of her tongue to tell him about her nursing experience, there was a positive longing to let him know that she hadn't been totally useless *all* her life. The thought of his approval suffused her body with a warm comfortable glow, but almost at once that was replaced by self-doubt. Wasn't it much more likely for his response to be a raised eyebrow, an implication that she couldn't stick it?

But before she had time to come to any decision the waiter returned to remove plates and the moment had gone. A bottle of wine was offered and approved and Carla touched the glass to her lips while Marc leaned his elbows on the table and stared across.

'And what about when your father remarries? Will that make any difference to you?'

'Remarries?' She tried to laugh, but the sound held more shock than amusement. 'There is no question of my father remarrying. He loved my mother and would never put anyone in her place.' Her voice trembled and she had the awful feeling that she was on the verge of tears.

'I'm sorry . . .' With an expression of embarrassment and relief he looked up as the waiter arrived with the next course and the conversation died while he bustled about, placing dishes in the centre of the table, polishing plates with a fresh napkin.

When he had gone, Marc made to refill her glass, but her swift shake of the head stopped him as much as the fact that she had scarcely touched the wine. 'Perhaps,' he poured some more for himself, a frown of concentra tion brought to the task, 'perhaps the wine isn't to your liking. Maybe you would prefer something . . . different?'

Carla glared at him, sensing that he had been on the point of offering something 'stronger' rather than different, then blushed as she remembered the other night and the scene in the corridor with Andrew. The pompous ass, he had thought she was drunk. How wrong could a man be? First that, then the even more ludicrous suggestion about her father.

'No, this is fine.' Studiously she avoided touching the wine, determined that she would do nothing to reassure him that she liked it.

The rest of the meal was taken in an awkward silence, broken only occasionally with inconsequential remarks which were almost more embarrassing than the silence. At last, with an air of thankfulness, Marc pushed back his chair, indicating his willingness to go and Carla led the way from the dining-room and stood on deck waiting for the boat that would take them back to where they had left the car.

'Why did you say what you did?' Before he could turn the ignition switch Carla turned to him fiercely. 'What possible reason could you have had?'

'About what?' His manner showed cool disdain.

His pretence did nothing to soothe, serving merely to increase her irritation. 'Oh you know perfectly well. Why did you say that Daddy intends to remarry?'

'Did I say that?' His voice was bland and expressionless. 'I don't . . .'

'You damn well know you did,' she interrupted before he could finish.

'I suppose it's because it seems the natural thing to do. He's still quite young. And attractive to women I should think. A man in his position is bound to find a wife an asset.'

'If it's so natural why are there so many unmarried men about? Yourself for instance?'

'Don't let's get on to me. That has nothing to do with what we're talking about. I just thought that perhaps your father might be lonely. It's some time since your mother died, I think.'

If there was a suggestion of sympathy in his voice Carla was too agitated to notice it.

'Lonely? Why on earth should he be lonely?' In the darkness her eyes blazed furiously at her companion. 'His work keeps him busy enough. And I'm with him most of the time.'

'I thought,' Marc's tone was irritatingly even, 'that you had just told me you travelled a lot. How long is it . . .' He turned away from her and switched on the engine '. . . since your mother died?'

'It's six years. Almost seven.'

'Then, surely you can see,' he negotiated the narrow twisting road skilfully, 'that he wants to share his life with a woman. It doesn't mean that his love for your mother is in any way diminished.'

'I'm not going to talk about it.' Although she stared straight ahead, she was seeing nothing.

'Very well.' There was a long silence which lasted until they hit the city again. Then as he began to head along Connaught Road, he flicked a glance in her direction. 'Will you come and have a drink with me before I take you home?'

'No thank you. Just drive to the hotel and I can finish the journey on my own.'

But when they reached the Mandarin Hotel, he drove straight past it, turning at the traffic lights and heading for the Peak. Carla didn't protest for she really felt incapable of driving herself. When they drew up outside the door of the villa, she asked, more out of habit than because she really wanted him to accept,

'Would you care to come in for some coffee? Then you can ring for a taxi.' Without waiting for an answer, she got out and walked to the house fumbling in her bag for her doorkey.

'Let me.' He took the keys from her trembling fingers then stood back, allowing her to precede him into the hall.

'There's the telephone.' She waved a vague hand towards the alcove beside the stairs, at the same time turning in the direction of the kitchen.

'Just a moment.' He caught hold of her arm and swung her round to face him. 'You and I have something to discuss and I won't be spoken to like a bell boy by a spoiled brat of a girl.' His voice was cold as steel.

There was a surge of triumph as she realised she had the power to make him show some emotion, she savoured it briefly before she drawled, 'But you just have, Doctor.'

Abruptly the fingers which had been pressing so painfully on her upper arms released her, but now it was the contempt of his gaze which hurt, which made her speak the words which brought such instant retaliation.

'And if you dislike me so much, I can't think why you wanted to go out with me this evening.'

'Wanted to go out with you.' The deep voice was now self-assured, amused. 'Why should you think I wanted it? It was obvious to me your father had some plans of his own, plans which excluded you, and that he was anxious that your evening should be arranged. That, my dear Miss Younger, is the only thing that would have induced me to embark on such an outing. Spoiled rich brats are just not in my line. Quite simply I was trying to help your father out. I like him and it seemed little enough to do when he has been so kind to me. But now,' his slight bow was mocking, humiliating, 'I consider I have done my duty. And the time has come to say goodnight.' He strode over to the front door, opened it, disappearing into the darkness of the night.

CHAPTER THREE

CARLA replaced the telephone with a faint smile of resignation. It looked as if she would have to accede to her father's suggestions. After all the turmoil and traumas of the last six weeks they had come to a fresh understanding and she was determined not to be the one to undermine that accord.

Her mind shied away from that last meeting with Marc Gérard, but there was no doubt everything that had happened since had seemed to stem from that time. Perhaps it was because there had been so many changes that his influence assumed an importance that was scarcely deserved. She was still smarting from the bitterness of his manner when her father had dropped his bombshell a few days later.

'I don't want you to be upset about this, Carla.' They were sitting on the terrace enjoying the coolness of the early evening when he had stretched out a hand across the table to cover hers.

Startled green eyes had shot open to stare at him in consternation. And in that instant she had known. What Marc Gérard had hinted at was no more than the truth.

'What is it, Daddy?' Her voice had sounded faint and distant.

'Joan and I are going to be married.'

'Joan?' For a moment the name brought no picture to her mind.

'Joan Christison. I think you like her. I know that she likes you.'

'Joan Christison,' she repeated the name stupidly. Then a sob had burst from her throat.

'Carla.' Her father's face had twisted with pain.

'Oh, it's all right, Daddy.' She had forced a smile to her lips. 'I'm not going to make a fuss. Only, it's a bit of a shock. I had no idea.'

'No.' He withdrew his hand and frowned down at his glass. 'Maybe that was a mistake. Only, we have been seeing each other a bit. First it was at other people's houses, at John Herbert's when you were abroad. We've always got on, you know. Even when James was alive. And we're both lonely.'

'Lonely?' There was an eloquent expressive question in the word so that she had no need to cry, as she had done before, 'Why on earth should you be lonely?'

Her father had sighed rather wistfully then. 'You won't understand, my dear. You can't unless you've been married, and happily married. I know you've done your best, but you couldn't take your mother's place . . .'

'But Joan can,' she interrupted swiftly, cruelly.

'No.' His voice was low. 'No-one can do that. No one person can replace another.'

'I'm sorry, Daddy. I do hope that you'll be very happy.' And she leaned over and kissed him. 'And I like Joan. I'm sure we'll get on together.' Her reward for that assurance was the sudden lightening of her father's face.

'I know you will, Carla. And it won't make any difference to *us*, to you and me. You know that, don't you?'

'Of course I do.' The cheerfulness of her voice hid the ache that was in her chest.

'I knew you would understand.' Mr Younger looked positively boyish. 'And you'll understand even more when you're married yourself.' He looked across at her roguishly. 'Any hope of you and Andy . . . ?'

'No hope at all, Daddy.' She could not have said what made her so definite, so final on that matter. But as soon as she had made the statement she knew that she would not change her mind.

'I'm glad, my dear He isn't the man for you.'

'I think you're right, Father.' She had dropped a quick, rather self-conscious kiss on the top of his head before going to her room. Only then had she found relief in a storm of weeping such as she hadn't given way to for many years.

Her first meeting with Joan had been awkward and not too friendly. It was difficult to avoid comparisons and this slight, rather negative woman was nothing like the glamorous image Carla had preserved of her own mother. But she was a *nice* woman and it was difficult to maintain an air of animosity. Besides, Carla had the distinct impression that if she did not adapt to the new circumstances it would be she who would feel the draught.

The thing that rankled longest and hurt her most was that she had been the last to know. Presumably if Marc Gérard knew that her father was thinking of remarrying then the entire staff of Younger Pharmaceuticals knew about it. She was hurt, but in the end the only thing she could do was shrug her shoulders, try to forget and accept the inevitable.

And over the weeks she had been able to see how her father changed, he relaxed and mellowed, planned little excursions for Joan and Carla, light-hearted outings of the kind that were normal enough in families. That in itself was difficult for Carla to accept, for it showed so demonstrably what had been lacking before. But now that she had become used to it, she couldn't regret the wedding which was due to take place in a month's time.

And now, her father with his new-found, light-hearted inspiration had rung her to ask if she would like to accompany Colin Jamieson on one of his delivery flights. She and Colin had known each other for years and although he was twenty years her senior she had cherished youthful romantic yearnings for him until he had suddenly married a Chinese girl when Carla was nineteen. At the time she had pretended to herself that her heart was broken, almost enjoying the drama of the situation while she moodily went about with a book of Shakespeare's sonnets in her hand.

But she had recovered fairly quickly, especially when she had met Lin, the exquisite little girl whom he had married. Now the couple had a son called Jamie and Carla was one of his godparents, although she saw less of them now than she would have liked as they had moved far out on the Kowloon side to live.

Less than ten minutes after her father had rung her with the suggestion, the telephone rang again and she wasn't surprised when Colin's exuberant Australian voice came to her over the wire.

'Carla? How are you?' Then without waiting for an answer, 'Why don't you ever come out and see us. You're missing the best of your godson, you know.'

'Yes. I'm sorry. Tell Lin that I'll be over next week some time. But I'll give her a ring.'

'Do that. But your father tells me that you'd like to come with me to the islands. Be like old times.'

'Yes.' She laughed. 'Remember how I used to pester you when I came home in the holidays. You must have been bored stiff.'

'I never was. And I won't be tomorrow if you'll come. Be at the airport at six. I won't wait for you, mind.'

And so the next morning at five to six, Carla drove out to the airport, shivering slightly at the earliness of the hour as well as the brisk little wind that was coming, mist laden, off the sea.

'Good girl.' Colin came striding towards her in the terminal building, bending to brush her face with his lips. 'Even at this unearthly hour you're worth looking at twice. But I'm glad you're well wrapped up.' He looked approvingly at the navy trouser suit and scarlet blouse which she was wearing. 'Paris clothes?' He raised an eyebrow as he led her over to where the small executive jet with the distinctive Younger black and gold flashing was waiting for them on the tarmac.

Half an hour later, they were banking steeply after take-off, then heading out over the top of the cloud, dodging dizzily for a moment among the crowding skyscrapers before turning south over the aquamarine ocean that lay beneath them. Carla sat up front with the pilot, not speaking till the hazards were safely behind them so they could relax and undo their seatbelts.

'Coffee?' She reached behind her for the bag of food she had brought with her.

'Thanks.' Colin searched in the pocket of his shirt for a

cigarette, lit it and drew the smoke, deeply, satisfyingly into his lungs. 'Now . . .' He put out a hand for the steaming cup she had put down on the ledge. '. . . Tell me what you've been doing? How was it in the States? And Europe?'

'They're still there.' She made a little face. 'The same as ever. London's a little shabbier, that's all.'

'Hmmm.' He blew the smoke down his nostrils and studied her through blue eyes. 'No young men? I thought you would have met at least half a dozen waiting to gobble you up.'

'Oh . . . There was a Lord or two. And a Marquis. But you know how it is. When your heart was broken at nineteen, it's not easy to make do with second best.' She had accused him often of being the reason for her unmarried state.

Colin chuckled, glancing down to check his direction on the Pratas Reef which foamed whitely beneath them. 'I can just imagine what your father would have said if I had told him I had designs on his daughter. No, honey . . .' The searching eyes looked towards the far horizon, 'he would not have been thrilled with the idea of a glorified taxi driver as a son-in-law.'

'Oh Colly . . .' Indignation caused her to relapse into her old familiar name for him. 'Daddy likes you a lot. I know that.'

'Sure he does. But he wouldn't have if I had married his daughter. Besides . . .' He grinned at her and thrust one powerful hand through his thick hair, 'I'm an old man, getting grey. Didn't you notice?'

'No,' she lied, although it was almost the first thing that she had seen when they met. 'But in any case, it suits you. Makes you look more distinguished. And you know I've always preferred the older man.'

'What about Andy?' Although Carla wasn't looking at him she was aware of his quick discerning glance. 'Are you still seeing him?'

'Yes.' She sighed, glad enough to be able to discuss the matter with him. 'But not so much in the last few weeks. Daddy doesn't approve of him either. And from most people's view, he could be an ideal match.' When he didn't at once agree with her she looked round at him. 'Don't you think so?'

Colin busied himself with the instruments for a moment. Then, 'Most mothers might think so. He's rich enough certainly. But . . .'

'But?' she prompted.

'But, cash is one problem that needn't worry you.'

'That's almost exactly what Daddy said.' She felt a prick of irritation. 'It's the first time I've known money to be such a positive disadvantage.' She sat staring ahead of her for a minute, noticing vaguely that the weather was showing signs of change. She leaned forward; looking down to the tiny cluster of islands over which they were flying, seeing the lash of an angry sea turning the aquamarine to a foaming white spume.

'It's blowing up a bit.'

'Mmm. Just a bit.' Colin's manner was unconcerned. 'But we haven't far to go.' He searched into his pocket for another cigarette. 'Got any more coffee in that bag? And I could do with a sandwich.'

But half an hour later a frown pulled Colin's eyebrows together and the sandwich lay uneaten on the ledge of the cockpit. He had fastened his seatbelt and had told

Carla to do likewise and they both sat looking out anxiously as squalls of tropical rain threw themselves against the glass.

'Thank God.' There was a sigh of relief as Colin turned briefly towards his passenger with a gleam of teeth. 'Dalaoa dead ahead. I was beginning to wonder if we had missed it. The head wind has delayed us more than I thought.'

'Dalaoa.' Carla spoke the name thoughtfully, certain that she had heard it before but not quite sure where.

'Yeah. I've got some boxes of some new drug for the doc on the island. Some World Health boffin. I heard he was in HK last month but I never met him myself. Guy called Gérard. You know him, Carla?'

The girl tried to control the chilly trembling that began to shake her limbs, her lips were stiff as she answered, 'Yes, I think I know him.' Her eyes were fixed on the tiny crescent of sand that fringed one side of the small island. Away to the right, on the horizon, lay the main archipelago of the North Gauran group, but Dalaoa was cut off from the rest by a coral reef which formed a wide circle about the island and could be seen quite distinctly from the air. She looked up at Colin, understanding that he was waiting for an answer to something he had said.

'Sorry. I wasn't listening.'

'Hey. You look worried.' He shot her a concerned glance. 'No need, you know. The weather's not as bad as all that.'

Carla had no inclination to tell him that the weather was the least of her concerns. 'I'm not worried about the weather. I'm just wondering where you land.'

'Don't worry, love.' He grinned at her, then began to

bank steeply for the descent. 'The island is bigger than you think. I've only been here once before. About nine months ago that was. I was told to head for the tallest palm tree on the island, travel east along the river until I reached the clearing and land there. See . . .' He pointed as he caught the gleam of water through the tops of densely planted palm trees. '. . . Now we are just . . . going . . . to put the wheels . . . down . . . Now!'

Carla felt the bump as they touched the not altogether smooth ground, saw the trees flashing past them, heard Colin grunt as he pulled on the brakes, then the tiny aircraft came to a halt at the farthest edge of the small clearing.

She gave a slightly shuddering sigh and turned to him with a smile that had the merest shade of tension. 'Nice landing.'

Colin grinned at her as he switched off the controls. 'It's all in the day's work.' Then his face grew more serious. 'You all right, Carla? Not airsick or anything?'

'No, of course not.' She lowered her head to release the seat belt and at the same time to hide her face from his perceptive eyes. 'It wasn't that bumpy.' Her self-assurance returned, enabling her to smile at him. Why should she feel nervous just because she was going to meet someone who had been insufferably rude to her? If there was any awkwardness then he should be the one to experience it. 'Is Dr Gérard expecting you?'

'No. At least yes. And no.' Colin clambered down, stretching out a hand to help his passenger. 'He knows that we'll be bringing the stuff, but not exactly when. I expect he'll have heard the engine.' He stood for a moment, eyes narrowed against the sun, staring towards the far side of the clearing. 'I'll get those boxes sorted out.'

While Colin clambered back into the plane, Carla rummaged in her bag for the sun glasses which would give her some protection from the unfriendly native when he appeared. It crossed her mind that she ought to be angry with her father for tricking her into this trip without saying exactly where she was going. He *must* have known. Could he have had any ideas . . .

No, surely not. And strangely enough she found she wasn't angry. Not *angry*. Excited. Stimulated. Perhaps it was because she had thought so much about Marc Gérard since their last meeting. It would be interesting to see if he measured up in the flesh to the importance he had assumed in the abstract. It would be a great relief to find the meeting an anti-climax. Then she could put him out of her mind and get on with her own life.

'Ah, there he is.' Colin's voice from above her head made her turn in the direction he had indicated. And there, coming towards them across the clearing, walking with that particular easy stride, casually dressed in khaki drill slacks and white shirt, was Marc Gérard. 'Hi doc.' As soon as he was within earshot Colin called out his greeting but did not pause in his work of positioning the various boxes for unloading. 'Got one of your boys about?'

'Hello, Colin. Yes, I think so.' While he spoke his eyes were rivetted on Carla's tall elegant figure as if even his dependable rational mind might be playing whimsical tricks.

Apparently struck by the lengthening silence, Colin glanced up quickly. 'You two do know each other, don't you?' He jumped down and leaned inside for the nearest box. 'Dr Gérard, Carla Younger.' He turned to face them. 'I thought you said you knew each other, honey.'

'Yes, we do.' With what appeared to be an effort Marc Gérard took his eyes away from the girl's. 'How do you do, Miss Younger.'

'Hello.' Her voice was low and sounded gauche, childish. But what distressed her most was the unexpected warmth in her cheeks, the hammering of her pulse.

'Then maybe if you could both take some of these packages, they aren't heavy at all, we could go along to the bungalow, doc, and needn't wait for the boys. Strikes me that you have some communications problems with the workers.' He glanced sardonically at the doctor.

Carla was surprised to see Marc Gérard laugh at the feeble joke.

'You could be right.' He stretched out for two of the packages. 'Come on, I was just going to have a drink. There's a can of beer if you don't mind going down to the waterfall to hitch up the basket.' He turned towards the track that meandered across to the far end. 'Can you manage, Miss Younger.' The glance at her red sandals suggested what he thought of her footwear.

'Yes. I'm fine.' She smiled sweetly as she lifted the parcel Colin had put beside her on the wing and followed them.

The small bungalow which was Marc Gérard's home, although a ramshackle affair by any modern standards, was surprisingly adequate inside. They climbed a few steps to the verandah where two elderly rocking chairs invited them to dally and look at the view over the river as it snaked round three sides of the clearing.

But they were taken straight through to the main room, a large apartment with a plain wood dining table pulled up to the unglazed window and four chairs of assorted shapes and sizes placed about it. At the other end of the room two rattan chairs and a Victorian sofa which had seen better days completed the furnishings. The room looked clean and even as she noticed this, Carla caught sight of a girl's face peering through at them from a door which presumably led to the kitchen.

'You'll stay and have something to eat, of course. I'm sorry it won't be what you're used to,' he glanced sardonically at Carla as he spoke. 'I'm afraid Deena isn't much of a cook.' He raised his voice and called the girl's name and she came into the room, smiling but not looking particularly shy. She nodded while Marc gave her rapid instructions in some sort of dialect, but did not take her admiring eyes away from Carla's face.

'I suspect that the meal will be even more hit and miss than usual.' When the girl had gone back to the kitchen and according to the noise proceeded to throw pots and pans about, the guests were waved to chairs while Marc went to a small cupboard hanging on one of the walls. 'Tea is coming, but of course the water won't be ready for some time. Maybe you would like some sherry, Miss Younger.'

'If you'll excuse me,' Colin walked purposefully towards the door, 'I'm parched. So I'll go and get myself a can of beer from the waterfall. I remember where it was kept.' Carla heard him whistle as he ran down the steps, leaving her alone with Marc Gérard.

'Sherry, Miss Younger?' She thought that his mouth had tightened, his manner become more abrupt as if there was now no need to hide the animosity he felt for her.

'If it's possible, I would prefer some water.' She glared back at him.

'Deena.' As he called he put the bottle back inside the cupboard with a thump. Then as the girl came through to stand smiling in the doorway, '*Sui Mm koi.*'

'If the water is safe to drink of course.' Carla felt she must not allow him to imagine that she was intimidated.

'Quite safe. Much safer than in most cities.'

'Then I shall enjoy it.' She turned away from him and walked over to the door so that she could look out. 'Thank you.' She took the water from him when he came over to her but refused to look at him. It was cool and refreshing.

'Why did you come here, Miss Younger?' His voice was arrogant, demanding.

At the implication that she had sought him out, the green eyes behind the dark glasses shot open and she swung round to look at him incredulously. 'I hope you didn't think that I had come especially to see you, Doctor?'

'From what Colin said, you were well enough aware that I was here.'

'The first I knew of it,' she drawled, 'was when we were landing in the clearing. If I had known before, it wouldn't have made any difference one way or the other. It simply wouldn't have mattered,' she lied and had the satisfaction of seeing his eyes darken in anger. It was a relief when she heard the sound of Colin's feet on the steps and he came swinging towards them over the verandah.

'Am I looking forward to this.' He tossed one of the tins he held up in the air and caught it. 'I brought one for you too, doc,' he smiled and licked his lips. 'Excuse me if I don't wait.' And he pulled the tab from the can before he raised it to his mouth. 'That was good.' He wiped his mouth with the back of his hand and turned to look out over the river. 'Weather's changing. I can smell a storm coming.' He glanced enquiringly at Carla, his keen glance appearing to notice the faint flush on her cheeks. 'I wonder if we should cut the food and make a run for it?'

'Of course.' Carla rose at once from the chair. 'I'm ready whenever you decide.' She ignored their host who was, she knew, looking at her through narrowed eyes.

'I'll just go and wash up a bit.' With a clatter of feet on the boards, Colin crossed the verandah again.

'I don't know that it's wise to take off with a possible storm in the offing.' The words spoken with some reluctance brought her eyes up to his face.

'I have complete confidence in Colin. He's a good pilot.'

'Or, is it perhaps that you'd rather risk the storm than remain any longer in my company?'

She seized on his words with mocking delight. 'Come, Doctor. You can't have it both ways. First of all you accuse me of chasing you to the island. Now apparently I'm dashing off prematurely.' She laughed. 'I thought you would have been more than pleased to see me go.' Her smile disappeared abruptly and they were still glaring at each other when the sound of Colin's feet clattering brought them both self-consciously round to the door again.

'I was saying to Miss Younger, perhaps it would be more sensible to wait and see what happens about the weather. It would be mad to set off and be caught by a storm half-way between here and Hong Kong.'

'Yeah. I've been thinking about that.' Colin wrinkled up his face and squinted out through the door. 'I think it's beginning to pass. Okay.' He smiled at Carla as he came to his decision. 'We might as well wait. Besides, the Chairman wouldn't thank me for taking chances with his precious daughter. In any case, I know Carla will want to see your hospital doc, she's keen on that kind of thing. Take her along there and I'll be happy here with that other can of beer. I see you didn't fancy it.'

'All right. If you would like to come along with me, Miss Younger, then I can show you what we have done in the last two years.'

There was no way to avoid the demonstration without a fuss so Carla contented herself with glaring at Colin while following Marc down the verandah steps.

When she had first approached the little bungalow she had failed to notice, behind it and towards the trees, a further cluster of buildings in the shelter of the encroaching jungle. They were more native in style than the bungalow, simple as it was, with attap thatched roofs and walls that did not quite reach the ground. The first hut, and the largest, could be identified as the consulting room for there was a table and chair with an electric light bulb hanging overhead and against one of the walls a high examination couch. That there was none of the gleaming chrome and glass which typify most modern surgeries did not detract from its functional appearance and the floor strewn with clean dry vegetation looked as hygienic as possible under the circumstances.

'This is the consulting room.' Marc Gérard showed no sign of diffidence about his modest facilities. 'And through here is the dispensary.' He led her through to the adjoining hut which was smaller but equally clean and obviously in charge of the young man who stirred from the mat in the corner when the doctor and the visitor arrived.

'This is Omar.' Carla detected a reproving look in Marc's eye. 'He looks after the dispensary and helps me generally.' Omar smiled shyly and looked down at his bare feet. His skin was sooty black, his teeth gleaming and he was dressed in a clean shirt and khaki shorts.

'Hello, Omar.' Carla's greeting was rewarded by a shy glance from beneath long fluttering eyelashes before he resumed study of his toes.

'And this is our hospital ward.' There was a note of pride in the doctor's voice as he led Carla through into a hut similar to the other two but which was furnished with two low Indian-style charpoys, simple frames of wood interwoven with webbing, each with a small white pillow and a white cover lying folded at the foot.

'No patients?' She looked at him with a querying, impulsive smile.

'No.' His eyes lingered on her shining hair before moving to her eyes still concealed behind sun glasses. At the suggestion of laughter about his mouth, she was filled with sudden pleasure. 'And it isn't that I've killed most of them off. It's simply that there's a festival in one of the villages and most of my patients refused to miss it.

They don't have the same respect for medical knowledge that we're used to in Europe. If they want to go, they just disappear. Then when it suits them they simply come back in the night, lie down on their beds and allow me to go on with my tests.'

'Tests? Then you aren't here only to look after them?'

'I hope I'm doing a little of that as well. The Japanese occupied the island during the war, that incidentally is how my bungalow came to be where it is, but since then time and progress have passed the islanders by. Not that I'm necessarily saying that's a disadvantage. But now I've managed to send one of the brighter young men, Omar's brother as it happens, to China to take a look at their village medical schemes. That should be a great advantage to them.'

'And you?' She enquired as they walked back across the clearing in the direction of the bungalow.

'Oh, I've been here to find out why the incidence of leukaemia is so high. I've specialised in the disease since I qualified and it seemed an opportunity to look at it from a different angle, in this unusual sort of closed society.'

'And have you? Found out why it's so common?'

'I shan't be able to say till all the notes have been collated. And until I can study the results of all the slides I sent back to Switzerland. But I have the feeling that perhaps they will only confirm what we already know. It's confined to one broad age group and that points to some slight but accidental release of radioactive material.'

'So, maybe you feel you have wasted your time.'

'No,' he gave a short laugh, 'strangely enough I don't. Does that sound amusing to your ears, Miss Younger?'

She was stung by the taunting note that had come back to his voice. Stung and hurt. 'An ambitious doctor should be making his way in his profession, not wasting time with people and places that don't matter.'

'You said that, Doctor. Not me.' Her voice trembled with anger then she turned to run up the short flight of steps to where Colin was leaning against an upright, studying the sky thoughtfully.

Lunch was a taut little meal which Carla's deliberate silence did nothing to alleviate. Once or twice she saw Colin dart reproving little glances in her direction, but she pretended not to notice them. Instead she went on eating the indifferently cooked rice and vegetables, determined that Marc Gérard would not have the opportunity to apologise that the cooking did not come up to the Peking or the Lisboa.

'Well,' Colin rose and stretched himself with an air of relief. 'That was okay, doc. Tell Deena from me that she isn't all that bad a cook.'

'I'll tell her.' Marc threw down his napkin with an alacrity that was just short of rudeness. 'If you must be off.' He walked with them to the verandah and stood looking over his domain. 'It does look more settled now.'

And it was true. The sky had the intense blue normal in the tropics in the early afternoon. A stillness hung about the trees, the birds were silent in the heat and the only sound that broke the quiet was the ripple of the water as it gurgled over the stony bed of the river.

'Then we'll leave you, doc. I suppose you'll be going to have a lie down on the charpoy for an hour. I don't mind telling you that's what I'd be doing if it wasn't that duty calls. Anyway we can see ourselves to the plane. So long. And thanks for the meal.' Colin turned to lead the way back to the clearing.

'Goodbye, Doctor. Thank you.' Carla turned to follow.

'Carla.' Her heart bounded as he spoke her first name. Until this moment they had been so formal with each other.

'Yes?' She turned with an impetuosity that she at once regretted.

'Thank your father for letting me have these drugs so quickly. And tell him I'll let him know the results.'

She waited. Then when he showed no sign of saying anything more personal, she turned away. 'I'll tell him.' She was brief and cool.

But as she followed Colin along the winding jungle path, there was a knot of sheer misery in her chest. And she wished that her reaction to Marc Gérard could be as cool as her words.

CHAPTER FOUR

'Say, what goes on between you two?' They had been airborne for only a few minutes when Colin turned to her with an enquiring look.

'What do you mean?' Carla tried to raise herself from the unaccountable despondency that had enveloped her. 'Between Dr Gérard and myself, do you mean?' she asked, knowing exactly what he was talking about.

'Sure that's what I mean,' his tone was dry. 'I've never seen you in such a tetchy glaring mood before.' He spoke with the frankness of an older brother. 'It was bad enough when I saw you giving *him* those condescending cold looks, but what did *I* do?'

'Oh, Colly.' To her dismay her voice trembled and the swift sting of tears made her blink. She bit her lip fiercely. 'You didn't do anything. You were just the pig in the middle.'

'Well thanks very much. That makes me feel a whole lot better.'

In spite of her depression, Carla giggled, a weepy watery sound.

'Good.' Colin cast an approving glance at her. 'I hate to see you so down, honey. You're the one person who never used to suffer from the usual feminine ups and downs.'

'Now I should thank *you*.' Carla laughed. 'That makes me sound like one of the boys. Very flattering.'

'I didn't mean that.' Colin's hand came across and squeezed hers. 'There's no-one more wholly female than you are. But,' he hesitated while casting an eye towards some dark clouds racing across the sky, blotting out the sun, 'I noticed it first thing when we met this morning. You seem to have lost some of your zest. That's why I asked about your holiday. I wondered if you had had a love affair that had gone sour on you.'

'No, of course not.' Against her wishes the memory of Marc Gérard thrust itself into her mind. 'Maybe I'm just a bit tired. Too much racketing around. I must remember I'm not so young as I used to be.' Then with a deliberate change of subject which told Colin pretty clearly that she had confided as much as she intended, 'I don't really like the look of the weather, Colin, do you?' A tiny niggle of worry was making her feel uncomfortable.

'No.' Colin's answer was revealingly brief and there was a tightness about his mouth as he looked at the black clouds that stretched from immediately above their heads to the distant horizon. 'Put on your safety harness, love.' Even as he spoke and reached for his own belt, a jagged fork of lightning cut brilliantly through the blackness of the sky, thunder crashed threateningly about them and the small plane gave a sickening lurch.

Carla saw Colin's knuckles gleam white as he wrestled with the controls while the storm growled and flashed about them with terrifying intensity. It seemed a long time before he spoke, although in fact it was no more than a couple of minutes. 'It seems pretty dark ahead,' he sounded calm, casually confident. 'So, I don't think we're going to run out of it so very quickly The sea looks pretty fierce too.'

'Yes.' Although she had already noticed that the sea was wild and angry, Carla glanced down again at the dark sullen water. 'Yes, it's quite a storm.' She spoke casually, determined to show none of the anxiety she was feeling. 'But it can't get any worse.'

As if determined to prove her wrong, there was another brilliant flash of lightning which she saw crack along the wings of the plane with terrifying force. Carla held onto her seat in an attempt to brace herself against the sickening jolt as the plane dropped into an uncontrolled spin. She sensed rather than saw Colin's struggle to regain authority over the machine, she heard him grunt with the effort, then gradually, blessedly, his efforts showed signs of success, the plane was pulled out of the wild descending spiral.

To her terrified eyes, the grey, storm-lashed surface of the sea was merely a few feet beneath the fuselage when at last they regained a straight course. She looked round at Colin, expelling a shuddering breath, noticing without surprise the knotted veins on his forehead, the perspiration running down his face.

'Good on you, Colin.' She gave a shaky little laugh. 'I hope you've got a life raft on board.'

'In the rear locker,' he replied with more plainness than she welcomed. 'But I don't know how long it would last in these seas.' Then he grinned at her briefly. 'I think the best thing we can do is head back to your friend in Dalaoa. With the gas we have we'll never make it in this storm. Or maybe you'd prefer to take your chances in the life raft.'

'No.' Carla shivered slightly. 'I don't mind where we go right now, so long as we reach land.' The waves beneath seemed to exert an awful fascination on her. She dragged her eyes away. 'I didn't bring a swimsuit.'

'Right.' Carefully, Colin brought the nose of the plane round, gradually gaining a little height then heading back in the direction from which they had come. Carla let out a shuddering little sigh of relief and fixed her eyes on the horizon, searching anxiously for that tiny blob that would tell them land was in sight.

Later, she thought that it was the longest half hour she had ever known. It was difficult to believe that the sea over which they were flying was the very same stretch of water which had smiled and glittered beneath them on the outward trip. Now it was as dark and forbidding as ever the Atlantic or the North Sea could look with that livid sullen colour which only tropical waters seemed to assume and which was even more menacing, more threatening than any in temperate climes.

And beneath that ugly heaving surface dangers more terrifying than even the elements lurked, ever-ready to threaten the unlucky or the fool-hardy. Carla felt a trickle of ice at the nape of her neck run chillingly down her spine. Sharks. The very name had always been enough to make her feel panic. But now, looking down at the sea she could imagine even more scary monsters, veiled and sinister, watching the progress of the puny ineffectual machine as it struggled to reach land and safety.

With an effort she wrenched her eyes up and away from the menace of the sea, searching the darkened sky for the outlines that would tell them that they were within sight of safety. And at last, slightly to their left, the elusive little shapes came blurrily into view. She sat back in her seat with a sigh of relief and a half-hearted grin for Colin who was frowning ahead into the diminishing light.

'Thank goodness.' Her voice was light, almost gay, as if the prospect of being thrown back into contact with Marc Gérard was one that had no terrors for her after what they had passed through.

'Hold on tight.' Colin spoke through gritted teeth as another ferocious squall took hold of the plane, tossing it first up, as a juggler might capriciously throw a ring into the air, then down to be caught carelessly before being discarded in a sideways gesture of contempt.

Carla sensed rather than saw the foam breaking on the shingle rocky beach on the north side of Dalaoa as the plane hurtled towards the water, impelled by the wind in a wild sideways direction. She closed her eyes as the trees came rushing towards them, then sat grimly, her spine pressed hard back into her seat as she anticipated the inevitable impact. And when that didn't come, when she heard an exhalation from Colin which might have been relief, experimentally she opened her eyes the merest slit.

They were skimming along the coastline now, apparently under control, but a brief glance showed Colin sitting forward in his seat, his face streaked with sweat, the intense blue eyes searching desperately in the vanishing light for the tall tree that would give them some guide to the landing area.

'Dead ahead.' His yell made her heart leap hammering into her throat and following the direction of his pointing finger she saw it, at the same instant feeling the plane bank wildly as he tried to bring the nose round for the landing.

The ground was almost swallowed up in darkness and bursts of tropical rain which the wipers could do little to clear, but even as she held her breath Carla knew that this was their only chance.

'Hold on, honey.' Colin's voice was perfectly calm, almost laconic as he fixed his position, veered slightly then came in over the tree tops, heading for the tall marker. 'I think we're going to make it.'

And they so very nearly did. Only at the very last was there a sudden capricious change of wind so that the huge primeval trunk of a tree which had been distorted with the pressure snapped back as if at the whim of a malevolent spirit. The crack as it caught the edge of the wingtip jarred along Carla's spine, whirling the machine in a wild crazy spin.

Afterwards it was difficult to decide exactly what happened. She remembered only clinging to the bucket seat, hearing a keening scream of fear or distress, but whether she had uttered it or whether it had been simply in her mind she was never sure. Foolishly her hands scrabbled at the fascia in a futile attempt to control the papers as they tumbled from the shelves to dance about the interior in a miniature snowstorm. Small pieces of equipment, the contents of her handbag, all joined the bits and pieces as they rattled about.

Inevitably, at the same moment as a jerk almost severed her head from her body, came the sound of tearing metal as the plane ripped through the treetops, the awful splintering of wood as branches were wrenched off. And then at last the stillness, the awful stillness as they came to a halt suspended at a crazy angle, like a toy aeroplane irretrievably trapped.

For an instant she might have lost consciousness. But almost at once realisation of bruising and shock brought her back to the present. Gingerly she moved her neck, relieved to find that despite the aches which appeared to have invaded every bone in her body, there seemed to be no serious damage. Tentatively she raised one hand to explore the source of pain on her temple and found a lump the size of an egg. But before she had time to do more than wonder at its size and tenderness a brilliant flash lit up the small clearing, reminding her of a more imminent danger. Even though they might be low on fuel it would take the merest spark to ignite the machine which would make the providence that had protected them so far seem less benign.

'Colin.' She forced herself to speak calmly while she tried to turn towards him, surprised to find that the position of the plane made it so awkward. 'Colin.' Pushing her head with one hand she found his figure, half-hanging from his seat harness in a position even more uncomfortable than her own. And there was just enough light to make out a dark smear on his forehead and even as she stared something warm and sticky touched her hand. 'Colly.' His name came out in a swiftly suppressed sob.

Everything became difficult in this situation, even the comparatively simple tasks like releasing the buckle of the safety harness. While she struggled with it, muttering softly beneath her breath, Carla's mind was absorbed with the possibility of fire, her ears were straining for the tell-tale crackling sound and her other senses were wildly alive to any signs of danger.

When at last with a protesting little click her seat belt slipped into the open position she levered herself out with a brief prayer of thankfulness. Before turning her attention to the pilot she reached out and turned off the ignition, grateful for the immediate lessening of her tension.

A brief examination of Colin's position made it clear that there was little she could do on her own. If she did succeed in releasing him from his harness he would merely slip from his seat with the possibility of further injury. There seemed no way that she would be able to hold him while she manoeuvred him into a position where it might, just might be possible to get him out of the plane. Colin was a pretty big man and lowering him to the ground in his present inert condition would need one or two strong men with a rope. No, the only thing she could do was to fetch help. She felt a tiny shiver run through her. She must get help. That was the only way to get Colin out of this topsy-turvy plane.

But even that was easier said than done, for the crash had obviously distorted the door so that it seemed immovable in its metal frame. Easing herself over the almost perpendicular tilt of the floor, Carla searched in the debris for the cosmetic bag which had spilled from her handbag and which held a nail file and a pair of scissors. It took ages before her fingers encountered the familiar shape and with a sigh of thankfulness she edged her way back to the door where she tried levering the tongue of the lock with the small tool. And when the file bent like a piece of tin she threw it away from her with a childish cry of rage.

She had been sitting sobbing angrily, despairingly for a few moments when she remembered what should have been obvious enough from the beginning. The plane had two doors. And in an instant change of mood she decided it was more likely that the other door would have escaped damage for it was her side which had received the full force of the blow.

Gradually, with difficulty, she managed to reach up towards the handle of the door close to Colin's dangling figure, straining to pull the lever into the open position. For a bleak endless instant she imagined it too had jammed, then with a little more exertion it slipped back smoothly.

Even then it was no easy task to pull herself upwards and out through the gap. Each movement rocked the tiny craft perched so precariously among the branches, so that she held her breath, her heart thumping with the urgency of her mission. The wind caught at her whenever her head emerged from the cabin, her feet slithered as they tried to find some invisible hold on the slippery outside skin of the plane. But she clung doggedly, her eyes searching frantically in the gloom for some means of reaching the ground.

It was some relief that they had come to rest on some of the lower branches of the tree. If they had settled on the top . . . She shuddered, wondering what it would have been like to spend the night, perched so high above the ground and with every fresh gust threatening to bring them crashing to the ground and certain oblivion.

No, she decided, she must be positive and realise how very lucky she was. Things could have been a great deal worse. They had escaped the ocean, they had survived the crash and if only she could get some help for Colin . . .

In the end the descent from the tree was easier than she had anticipated even though it happened more by accident than by any decision she had made. Quite simply she lost her balance when a branch gave way under her weight and found herself sliding down till she was trapped in a split in the main trunk. Then by clinging to one of the tendrils which hung like ropes she lowered herself to the ground with a bump.

She lay for a moment on the ground, faintly sickened as the jarring pains took over her body again, just vaguely conscious of an especial ache in her shoulders, that her palms were stinging from friction burns. But almost at once she got up, realising for the first time she had no idea which direction to take. They had come down just a short distance from their first landing point, that much she knew. But in all the confusion she had lost her sense of direction and in the dark it was unlikely that she would recognise any landmark which would give her a clue.

For what seemed like hours she squelched about, slithering in the mud which a short time before had been ground dry and baked hard with the sun. Before she left the spot where they had come down she tied a hand-kerchief to a bush and when she found she had come back to it for the third time, despair and hopelessness made her long to find a corner out of the wind where she could just lie down and give up.

And then, almost accidentally, she found the path. Now it was more like a rutted stream and she had even begun to retrace her steps, convinced that she had made another mistake when a sudden brief flash illuminated something that caught at her memory. She hesitated and even as her head told her she was making a mistake she turned her feet along through the trees, certainty mounting inside her at each step so that she tried to hurry in the slippery mud, her breath sobbing from exertion and strain.

Her sodden clothes were clinging to her, an ankle which she didn't know she had wrenched was beginning to ache more persistently and her whole body seemed to be overwhelmed with cold and misery. The wind tore at her relentlessly, plastering her hair to her face in long wet strands.

Desperation began to mount again, to stifle any confidence that she had found the path to the bungalow when ahead of her and slightly to the right something glimmered through the dim aqueous gloom. It appeared and disappeared as she forced her way through bushes, but all the time it grew stronger so that at last there was no reason to temper her optimism any further.

Thank God, she thought as she came out into the little clearing and saw the uncurtained windows spilling their faint light into the surrounding darkness. Thank God. A sob caught in her throat and she found the strength to run, her feet in their elegant red sandals slipping on the water-logged turf.

With her hands on the rail she pulled herself up the steps to the front door, hearing with a strange detachment the sounds which came echoing through the window. On the top step she paused, pushing the hair back from her face with one shaking hand. The music was a tune she knew well enough. Or she had known it when she was a child. It was one which her parents had loved. Vaguely she knew that it came from a show, the first show her father had taken her mother to see. They had met on his first leave home and he had taken her to see *Oklahoma*.

Now, an unknown tenor warbled scratchily, reminding Carla that they had never played it after her mother's death.

> 'Don't throw bouquets at me,
> Don't please my folks too much,
> Don't laugh at my jokes too much,
> People will say we're in love.'

Carla put out her hand, pushing at the door, but it refused to give way. In the dark she sought the handle and that too refused to yield. Tears began to join the rain on her face, streamed down into her mouth as she wondered if she were in some terrible nightmare. Perhaps she wasn't on Dalaoa Island at all but some other place, inhabited by ghosts of the past.

Hopelessly now she beat on the door panels with clenched fists, her weeping face sinking onto her breast in a gesture of despair. 'Marc, Marc,' she cried silently, 'where are you? Why aren't you coming to help me?'

And then miraculously the door opened, light streamed out onto the verandah, strong hands were lifting her to her feet.

'Carla. Thank God.' Marc's hands were holding her, pulling her to him. Then he was lifting her in his arms, carrying her into the peace and safety of the bungalow.

CHAPTER FIVE

FOR a long time Carla lay in the blissful comfort before her mind was willing to think of anything that had happened the previous day. It was perfect simply to lie watching the slatted pattern of light where the sun streamed through the rattan blinds. Outside she could hear the calling of a hoopoe, the soft gibber of a monkey from a tree close to her window. She closed her eyes again, drifting for a moment back towards sleep, a smile touching the soft mouth.

Then quite abruptly her eyes shot open and she sat up in the wide bed. His pyjamas. She was wearing his pyjamas. And where had he slept she would like to know? Fearfully she looked at the pillow close to her own and it was almost a surprise to see it so plump and pristine. Carla sank back into the warmth of the bed, trying to remember all that had happened the previous night.

After he had caught her to him, murmuring soothing little endearments into her soaked hair, he had put her into a chair, looking at the bruise on her head, the weals on her palms with a tenderness that was hardly professional. He had fetched ice and while she had held it to her forehead he had smeared some soothing cream over her hands.

Dealing with her wrenched shoulder and ankle he had become more business-like, strapping the foot with a firm bandage, assuring her that the shoulder would benefit by a night's sleep, then listening with a frown of concentration when she went on to tell him about Colin and where the plane could be found.

Then he had hurried off and she heard him outside, calling to people before he reappeared for a moment, pushing a glass of whisky into her hand as he was about to leave her.

'I'll be back soon Carla.' He swung a rope about his shoulder, 'Omar and I will bring Colin back safely. Don't worry. And I've told Deena to come and heat water for you. She'll show you how to use the shower. Don't worry, everything will be all right.' But there had been no recurrence of the tenderness that he had shown in those first moments when he had held her, when he had seemed as emotional at their unexpected reunion as she was herself.

And later, hours later it seemed, when she heard them coming back she had run out onto the verandah, relieved to see that he and Omar were carrying Colin on a wicker stretcher.

'It's okay.' The face that he turned up to her was grey with fatigue. 'I think it's concussion and his shoulder is dislocated. I'm taking him to the hospital so that I can examine him properly.'

Carla waited in the house, but she stood by the window where she could see the flickering light from the surgery and occasionally a pair of legs could be seen passing between the light and the open sides of the building. She was lonelier than she had ever been in her life before and if it hadn't been for the storm, for the frightening way that strong trees were bent close to the ground, she knew that her need for human companionship would have driven her down the path towards the light.

For Deena had disappeared. She had shown Carla the little lean-to at the side of the house where a shower of sorts could be enjoyed, had demonstrated with ill-concealed impatience how to control the flow of warm water by pulling on an ancient lever and then had hurried off, banging the door of the outhouse behind her.

It had been bliss for Carla to strip off her sodden things and to stand with her face turned up to the cleansing stream. The soap in the little crevice in the side of the wall was functional and masculine, smelling faintly of carbolic, but after a moment's hesitation she used it, trying to ignore the intimacy of knowing whose body had been previously lathered by it.

On the inside of the door was a navy towelling dressing gown and after she had dried herself on the rough towels she slipped her arms into it and tied the belt firmly about her waist. She supposed it was *his*, but he could scarcely object to her borrowing it. At least he would prefer that to her going about naked, she decided with a nervous little smile, before opening the door of the shower-room and clinging to the wall where she could find a bit of protection from the wildness of wind and rain. She managed to find the verandah and leaned against the door with a sigh of content.

She had been standing by the window for some time before she realised that the bungalow was unnaturally quiet. Outside the storm still roared with unabated fury, but once the ears became accustomed to that it was impossible to ignore the suspicion that she was completely alone. Especially when she remembered the noisy way Deena had gone about preparing the meal which they had eaten earlier in the day. Carla went through the door which she knew led to the kitchen and found her suspicions confirmed. Under the dim light of the naked bulb which hung disconsolately from the ceiling it was evident that all the preparations for the evening meal had been abandoned quite suddenly.

On a chopping board in front of the window lay an onion, half-chopped, a few peppers waiting to be sliced and a bunch of rather tired looking spinach.

'Deena.' Carla raised her voice and called the girl's name. Then she repeated it, but the only answer was the wind which howled round the building with redoubled force as if underlining the fact that she was alone. She shivered, suddenly cold in the clammy heat, but a moment later her good sense reasserted itself. Why should she feel abandoned when at this very moment Marc and Colin were very likely to be on their way back to the bungalow.

And what, she reminded herself, would be the first thing that tired men would want when they came back. A meal. They would be weary and hungry and they would want some food. And it seemed that the only person who would be able to provide that was herself. So she had better get cracking. Otherwise her host, her reluctant host, would be very likely to tell her that while he had been working to release her pilot, the least she could have done was to provide them with something sustaining to eat when they got back.

Fired with an unexpected enthusiasm, Carla folded

back the sleeves of the robe which kept falling over her hands. A quick look round the kitchen showed a tiny refrigerator throbbing restlessly in one corner and when she opened it she found two chicken legs. Another cupboard revealed a supply of rice stored in a huge insect-proof tin and the usual sauces and seasonings.

The stove was an ancient oil contraption, the fuel supply suspended in a glass jar at the side of the burners and Carla, who hadn't seen this kind of cooker since her childhood, was relieved to see that it was well-filled. One of the two burners was used for the pot of water in which she would cook the rice and on the other she placed a wok ready for stir-frying the chicken and vegetables when the men were almost ready to eat.

Nevertheless she still had almost an hour to wait until she could produce the meal and contrary to what she had visualised she and Marc sat down alone to eat. She felt unaccountably disturbed as she brought in the dishes and put them in the centre of the table where they hid the stains of soy sauce from previous meals.

'Can I go down to see Colin later?' It was she who at last broke the silence between them and looked into the dark eyes which had been surveying her with such intensity. She had no intention of letting him see how she minded the abrupt change from the tenderness he had shown when she had come beating on the door after the accident.

'If you wish to.' Even as he stretched out a hand to take the plate of food which she held out, his eyes never left hers. 'Although I doubt if he'll be awake. I gave him something to make him sleep and I've put the fear of God into Omar so he'll be there all night.'

'Oh . . .' For no reason that she could think, colour flooded into her face and she looked down at her food, hoping to conceal her emotions from him. Only the tightness of her fingers round the fork prevented her hand from trembling and she stirred a little of the rice before raising it to her mouth.

'Mmm.' Marc threw down his napkin and got up from the table. 'This calls for something decent to wash it down.' She saw him go to a cupboard and emerge with a glass which he held up to the light before setting it down on the table in front of her. And in the other hand a bottle of wine. 'It's not château bottled I'm afraid, Miss Younger, but . . .' He strode off in the direction of the kitchen and came back with a cup. '. . . Perhaps you will make allowances.'

It was ridiculous to be hurt by him. In fact she ought to prefer him to call her Miss Younger. Only her friends had the right to use her Christian name and whatever he was, he had shown no inclination towards friendliness. And the implication was clear enough in his manner that she was a spoiled rich girl who would never drink anything but the finest wines.

'No thank you.' It gave her a great deal of pleasure to refuse him. 'I don't really drink a great deal.'

'No?' One eyebrow curved mockingly and he smiled as he poured some of the liquid into her glass. 'You surprise me.'

'I'm sure I do,' she answered crisply. 'But you don't surprise me, Dr Gérard. Not one little bit.'

'No?' He sat down opposite her, smiling as if he was happy now that he had provoked her, the dark grey eyes continuing to look at her as he raised the cup of wine to his mouth. 'Mm. Not bad. Try it, Miss Younger. I really would like your opinion. It's a little hobby I took up since I came to the island. I make it from pears and sugar.'

'You make it yourself?' She looked at him in horror. 'Then nothing would induce me to taste it.'

'Now how would you have felt if I had refused to eat the meal that you produced.'

'I would have felt nothing.' Angrily Carla loaded some of the rice and vegetables onto her fork and ate it, relieved to know how good it tasted. 'I don't care if you eat it or not.' She glared at him as she lied brazenly.

'Not only am I prepared to eat it,' he paused to put another forkful into his mouth and looked at her while he ate it. 'I admit quite happily that you are a better cook than Deena.'

Carla smiled sweetly and leaned her elbows on the table, cupping her chin in her hands. 'How kind of you. Especially when at lunch time you said what an awful cook she was.'

He shrugged, as if giving the point to her. 'Well, yes. Perhaps the competition isn't the fiercest in the world. But . . . still, I am surprised.'

'You know nothing about me so why should you be surprised?'

'I wouldn't say nothing.' All the laughter had gone from his face. He was grim and serious. 'One way and another . . .' the grey eyes were cold, '. . . I think I know a fair amount.'

At once Carla's mind went back to that first night, when they had met in the corridor of the hotel in Macao. Somehow she knew that was what he was thinking of and the conclusions he had drawn were only two obvious. Again she felt her cheeks grow warm, but this time, refusing to try to conceal the fact, she stared at him and held out a hand for his empty plate.

'Have you had enough?' Her voice was stiff with anger.

'No.' To emphasise his denial he shook his head and raised the cup again. 'No, I haven't.'

'Then,' more disturbed by his unwinking gaze than she could understand or explain, Carla pushed the dishes towards him. 'Have some more. There's . . . there's more in the kitchen. I saved some for Colin,' she stammered. 'And for Omar too if he wants it.'

'Thank you.' With an amused look on his face he put down the cup. 'But I shan't have any more unless you agree to try some of the wine. I'm sure you'll enjoy it,' he insisted.

'No. I told you, I don't drink,' she replied primly.

'And what was that you swallowed when you came into the bungalow this evening?' His voice was like a whiplash. 'I didn't notice any shrinking from alcohol then. Nor from anything else . . .'

Carla got to her feet, trying to ignore the weakness in the region of her knees, her hands clutching at the wrap which was threatening to part at the front. 'How dare you.' Her voice trembled and she was very close to tears. 'As far as the whisky was concerned, I thought,' she was pleased with the amount of scorn she managed to convey, 'I thought that was being prescribed for me by a reputable doctor. But perhaps,' the words tumbled over themselves in their hurry to be spoken, 'you have some other reason for trying to force me to drink.' The moment she said the words she regretted them and watched while he put down his napkin and rose lazily to his feet. He towered above her like some avenging angel. Or devil she amended with a tiny shiver of fear. A smile came and went about his mouth without ever reaching his eyes, but when his hand came out to touch her cheek she was unable to move away from it.

It lingered for a moment, making her clean skin feel silky and alluring, causing a shudder to rack her waiting expectant body, then it moved beneath the heavy fall of hair to the nape of her neck where it stroked sensuously. When he pulled her towards him, imprisoning her firmly against his chest where she could feel the hard fierce beating of his heart, she closed her eyes in anticipation of his kiss, raising her face to his.

The bruising mouth, the rough rasping feel of his skin against hers brought that trembling tingling sensation at the base of her spine exploding like a powerful drug in her bloodstream. She gave a soft little moan of surrender as she relaxed against him, willing his hands to mould her body ever more closely against his. Her resistance was a mere token before she allowed his searching lips to part hers while her hands linked about his neck in an endeavour to hold him ever more closely against her.

Then, just as she felt she would faint with the intensity of her pleasure, firm hands dragged at her, pulling her back from that torment of delight and sweetness. She moaned again, this time in uncomprehending protest, and her eyes opened reluctantly.

'You see, Miss Younger,' his face was white and the eyes had lost some of their self-control as he glared down at her. 'It takes two to make a bargain of the kind you were suggesting.' He looked down at her heaving breast and a faint smile came to his bitter mouth. 'Despite your words you don't show that you are exactly unwilling. However, please take my word for it that your,' he hesitated offensively, 'your honour is perfectly safe for as long as you stay on the island.'

The sob which escaped from Carla's lips infuriated her so much that she reached to the table for support and found the glass of wine which she had refused. Before she had time to think any more of what she was doing she had raised it, throwing the contents in Marc Gérard's face. She saw him flinch, then stand motionless while the golden drops dripped slowly, as if time were suspended, down his face, and splash onto his shirt.

'Besides,' it was a long time before he spoke and his mouth was a straight hard line over his teeth, 'you just aren't my type, Miss Younger. And I don't take other men's leavings.'

He caught the arm that came up in an arc destined for his cheek. 'And don't do that either,' he spat the words at her. 'So much I'm prepared to take from you . . . I make allowances for the spoiled little brat you are . . . But don't push me too far.' Then with a gesture that seemed to tear the skin from her wrist he threw her hand away from him.

It was impossible to say how long they stood there staring at each other. The atmosphere about them seemed to have a life of its own that had nothing to do with the storm but which encapsulated them, separated them from the reality of everything but the terrible destructive emotion they felt for each other.

Suddenly, Carla saw his head turn away and his body

moved with seeming reluctance towards the door. Only
then did she heard the sound of someone hammering
impatiently, heard a voice calling in through the louvred
shutters and recognised that Omar had come in search of
Marc. Her swift feeling of apprehension for Colin was
swiftly eased when, after he had listened to the boy's
explanation for a moment the doctor turned in her
direction with a weary gesture.

'It's nothing for you to worry about.' He spoke as if he
had sensed her reaction. 'Colin is perfectly all right and
sleeping peacefully. One of the villagers has been badly
cut by a piece of metal blowing around. I'll have to go
and stitch him up.'

'But you can't.' For the first time Carla realised how
exhausted he looked and her protest was instinctive, a
result of the overwhelming tenderness that unexpectedly swept through her as she noticed the dark shadows
beneath his eyes, the lines of fatigue about his mouth.

'Oh, you needn't worry.' She wondered if he chose
purposely to misinterpret everything she said. 'You'll be
quite safe here. I'd better show you where you can
sleep.' Without waiting for her to answer he turned and
led the way through a small inner hall and into a bedroom.

Carla looked round at the small room illuminated by
the low power bulb which dangled from the ceiling. Like
the rest of the house it was depressingly dull with an
old-fashioned chest of drawers against one wall and a
large bed dominating the confined space.

'But . . .' she hesitated. '. . . This is your room.'

'Yes.' He turned round from an impatient search
through one of the drawers. 'But what I said still goes.'

He tossed a pair of clean but not ironed pyjamas onto the top cover. 'You'll have to make do with this, Miss Younger. It's not the Lisboa, I know. But I can assure you that you'll be safer here than you were there.' And having delivered the final thrust, he turned and left her, closing the door behind him with considerable force.

Recollection of the previous evening's happenings came back to Carla as she lay watching the sunlight move about on the wall of the room. She found herself growing hot with rage and embarrassment as she remembered how she had melted into his arms at the first opportunity. And the contempt with which she had been rejected. Not that she was the least bit sorry about that. In fact it was the only relief in the whole embarrassing episode. For while it would be silly to deny that she had welcomed that little moment of relaxation in his arms, she would not have been prepared to go any further. No matter what, her reactions were the same as his. Marc Gérard, she assured herself firmly, just wasn't her type. She cursed the unusual slowness that had allowed him to get his gibe in first. How different she would have felt this morning if that part had been reversed. It would have been so satisfying to tell him just how important he was in her life. Now he was probably imagining that she had spent a frustrated night thrashing about on her, or rather his, lonely bed. Instead of which she had slept like a log.

But now, it was time to get up. She reached to the foot of the bed for the dressing gown which she had tossed down before switching off the light last night. The bungalow was quiet as she opened the door and tiptoed, bare-footed, across the hall and into the living-room so that she jumped when a voice wished her good morning and she turned round to see him sitting at the table.

'Good morning.' Defensively she pulled the dressing gown closer at the neck and then wished she had been less obvious.

'You slept well?' She sensed the mockery in his voice and glared at him. 'How are the shoulder and ankle?'

'Both fine. Thanks.' Then she coloured. 'I'm sorry, I had your bed. Where did you . . . ?'

'Oh you needn't worry about that, Miss Younger. There is another room in the bungalow and I used that.'

Still her guilt persisted although she couldn't help noticing that he looked remarkably fresh and relaxed after all the turmoil of the previous evening. The dampness of his hair indicated that he had already showered, his face looked smooth and shaven, the clean shirt and slacks contrasted with those he had been wearing last night. His sardonic expression told her that her scrutiny had been noticed and she slipped into the chair opposite him.

'I'm afraid we don't have the conventional breakfasts here, Miss Younger, but . . .'

'Oh for heaven's sake . . .' The words broke irritably from her lips before she could stop them and the look of condescending enquiry on his face made her feel even more scratchy, 'must we persist with this childish stupidity?' Her eyes flashed angrily. 'You know my name perfectly well and you're just trying to provoke me with this insistence on "Miss Younger".' Her hand reached for the coffee pot which he had pushed in her direction and she poured some into her cup, scarcely noticing that a little spilled into her saucer. 'And,' she lifted the cup, holding it between both hands to sip, 'I never eat in the mornings. Coffee is just fine.' She smiled nastily.

'Well, one thing isn't fine and that's your temper. I hoped that a night's sleep would have improved it but it seems I was wrong.' The mocking drawl persisted in his voice, but with a rapid change that robbed her of the opportunity of a snappy reply he went on to speak about his patient. 'Oh and Colin is feeling much better this morning. Omar has just been up for some food for him and when he gets up he seems determined to go for help.'

'For help? But . . .' She glanced out of the window towards the palm trees that were still being shaken about in the dying storm. 'But where can he go? It wouldn't be safe . . .'

He shot an amused glance towards her. 'I'm glad we agree on one thing at least. But . . .' He rose pushing his chair back and standing for a moment looked down at her. 'I suppose I can understand his problem. It's not the best way to help your career, taking the chairman's daughter out for a joy-ride and ditching her and the plane.'

'It wasn't a joy-ride,' she replied coldly. 'Colin was on a normal business flight and I came with him as I've done so often in the past.'

'Mmm.' There was a thoughtful expression on his face as he looked down at her. 'Doesn't Colin's wife mind you going with him on his business trips?'

'No.' She struggled to remain calm. 'Strange as it may seem to a person like you, Dr Gérard, I don't think she does. Not everyone shares your jaundiced view of human nature.'

'Mmm. As you say, strange!' Then with another abrupt change of subject, 'might I suggest you get dressed as soon as possible. I would be grateful for some help in the house.' His eyebrows came together in a slight frown. 'I'll get Omar to go along the village later and bring Deena back. She should have got over the shock of the storm by now but until then . . .'

'I . . .' Carla, remembering for the first time where she had left her wet clothes, felt her cheeks grow warm. '. . . I think I left my things in the shower room last night. I don't suppose they'll be dry . . .'

His eyes narrowed slightly and then a faint smile indicated that perhaps her actions were only what he would have expected.

'Of course,' he said sarcastically, 'I forgot that you're used to having a maid to lift up your clothes when you drop them. I ought to have remembered that and taken care of your clothes for you.'

She glared at him, but for the moment she could think of nothing sufficiently smart to crush him. Instead she tried to take refuge in attack. 'As you have obviously been in the shower you must have seen them and could have told me when I came in this morning.'

His steady stare had a tinge of contempt and deep down Carla cringed when she admitted that his attitude was justified, a feeling that increased when he answered.

'I had a shower in the waterfall at the river bend.' His tone was totally impassive as if he no longer felt any interest in what she said or did. 'I'll get you something to wear.' He turned and left the room.

A moment later he came back with a new pair of khaki drill trousers over one arm and a clean shirt. 'I'm afraid this is the best I can manage. I don't have any shoes that would fit, but you might find some of Deena's flip-flops in the kitchen.' He put the clothes down and turned to go.

'Can I . . .' Her voice stopped him. 'Can I come down and see Colin. I must try to persuade him to stay where he is for a day or two.'

'Yes. Come whenever you're ready. Although I doubt if you'll be able to change his mind.' He turned and walked out of the room.

When she went into the bedroom to change, Carla was conscious of a pain in her chest unlike anything she had ever experienced before and she was unable to hide from herself that it was all to do with Marc Gérard. It was a long time since she had met a man whose good opinion was important to her. And it was a cruel trick of fate that when such a man came along he should view her as a spoiled brat, the cruel bitter words he used could never be erased from her memory. The indulged only child of a rich man, a girl who found relief from the boredom of her butterfly existence at the gaming tables of Macao and the bed of any man who took her fancy. That was what he saw every time he looked at her.

Struggling to bring the waist of the trousers round her own slender figure she raised her head to see her image in the spotted glass of the mirror on the bedroom wall. The sad contrast between the Carla Younger who had just been in her mind, the glamorous socialite, and her present reflection could hardly have been greater. At other times she might have been able to laugh at herself, but just then she was too over-wrought, much too emotional to find any amusement in her situation. An involuntary hand went up to touch her hair, finding in the tumbled mass about her shoulders little to suggest her usual sleek well-groomed style. And his shirt and trousers which fitted her nowhere only added to her clownish appearance.

How well she could imagine Marc Gérard's reaction when he saw her. How pleased he would be to see her so humiliated. And he would be even more humiliated if the trailing inconvenient garments caused her to sprawl at his feet. But that at least she could and would prevent. In one of the kitchen drawers she remembered seeing a large pair of scissors and it would be the work of a moment to adjust the trousers at least as far as the length was concerned. And when she got back to civilisation it would give her a great deal of pleasure to send him a whole box of slacks to replace them.

She smiled with a grim satisfaction as she wielded the scissors inexpertly, determined to ignore the stinging that the effort caused on her rubbed palms. But when the job was done and she stepped into her Bermuda shorts she was further inspired to hack short the sleeves of his shirt and to tie what remained in a defiant, none too comfortable knot in front.

She studied her reflection with all the attention she was used to giving her purchases in the Rue St Honoré, then with her chin at a challenging angle she went out, prepared to take anything that Marc Gérard felt like throwing.

CHAPTER SIX

CARLA's heart was in her mouth as she watched the small canoe, an insignificant dot now on the turquoise blue water, make for the gap in the circle of foam boiling over the reef enclosing Dalaoa Island. From where she was sitting on the promontory above the bay it was easy enough to decide which way they should take, but she knew that from their vantage point at sea level, it would be much less obvious. She drew a deep gasping breath when she saw the small boat picked up by the power of the seething water, whirled about for a moment like a cork and then dropped. She closed her eyes, her mind saying a silent prayer before she opened them. Unable to see anything for a moment, she felt panic overtake her and then she sighed, a long expressive sound as she caught sight of the boat again, this time through the bar and battling forward into the strong swell of the open sea.

If only Colin had heeded the advice he had been given. Both she and Marc had pleaded with him to wait, for even another day, before making the trip to Mainland as the chief island in the group was called. But she had forgotten just how obstinate Colin could be when he had made up his mind.

'I'll be all right.' And he had grinned at her. 'And I know the doc will look after you till I get back.'

She had ignored that last remark, contenting herself

with a reproving look which she knew would have no effect on Colin, but concentrating on his bandaged shoulder and the bruise that disfigured his forehead. 'But it's ridiculous to go off in an open boat in your condition. You don't seem to realise that you were very lucky to survive a plane crash yesterday.' She emphasised the last word. 'Less than twenty-four hours ago.'

'Sure I realise that. And if it hadn't been for the way the doc strapped me up it would be a different story. But . . .'

'If I were the doctor I'd refuse to let you go.' They were sitting round the table drinking coffee after the meal which Carla had prepared for them and she skilfully avoided looking in Marc's direction when she spoke.

'Oh, don't blame Marc . . .' Colin shot a sardonic glance at the other man as he spoke, '. . . he's done his best to make me change my mind. But don't worry, honey.' He got up and put his uninjured hand on her arm. 'He's arranged for me to take someone who could find his way blindfold through the reef. All I have to do is lie back and let the other guy do the work. Then when I get to Mainland I can send a message on the two-way radio and in no time at all we'll have a plane here to take us off.'

Marc, who had been particularly silent during the meal, seemed obliged to drag his eyes away from that hand on her bare arm, he pushed back his chair so that its legs screeched over the bare boards of the floor and went to stand looking out of the window. 'At least the wind appears to be dropping now. With luck it won't take you more than two hours to reach Mainland and if you get your message through, then you could be back before dark.'

But he hadn't, as Carla half-hoped, come with her to watch the boat on the first part of its perilous journey. He had merely shown her the path she had to take through the undergrowth, had stood watching for a moment before turning back and striding over to the hospital.

When she could no longer see even a black dot on the surface of the water Carla rose with a sigh and retraced her steps. At least when she got back to the house she would be able to put on her own clothes. She had found a length of wire suspended between two trees at the back of the house with a few clothes pegs fixed onto it. It had been the work of a moment to retrieve her clothes from the shower room and to hang them out, pleased at the way they billowed in the strong wind. If only, she admonished herself, if only she had thought of doing something about them last night she wouldn't have had to humiliate herself in front of Marc Gérard. And probably there *was* something in his taunt about her never having to lift up anything that she dropped. It made her despondent even to think of it. And her childish reaction in cutting short the legs of his trousers hadn't even been noticed.

Carla wandered back through the undergrowth, scarcely aware of the fresh luxuriant green of the vegetation after the rain, stepping over a fallen tree without thinking about it, not even seeing a lizard which she disturbed as she stumbled against a boulder. Her mind was filled with the dissatisfaction that had troubled her for years, but now there was nothing vague about the feeling. It was insistent and clamouring for a solution. And she was certain that the answer was further away than it had ever been.

When she reached the bungalow she was relieved to hear from the clatter of pots in the kitchen that Deena was back. The girl greeted her with a shy smile and a few words that meant nothing to Carla. They both made signs to each other signalling relief that the storm had passed before Carla went to the bedroom with the bundle of dry clothes which she had retrieved from the line at the back of the house.

Feeling more confident now that a familiar reflection greeted her in the glass, Carla returned to the kitchen determined to keep herself busy until Colin returned. She was fairly certain that Marc would keep out of her way till evening and as there was nothing else to do she could at least try to show the girl some of the elements of cooking.

Using sign language and a few words of Cantonese which Deena seemed to understand, Carla began to assemble the ingredients for a vegetable curry. The lunch she had prepared had been limited by what was available and the result was three rather small omelettes served with slices of fried plantain. Followed by fresh pineapple it had been satisfactory enough, although scarcely in the gourmet class, but she felt that for the evening meal she could produce something slightly more ambitious. Not that she cared about Marc Gérard or what he thought of her. She was mainly interested in escaping from the boredom of doing nothing.

She was so busy searching in the small cupboard for

recognisable ingredients that she didn't at first hear someone at the kitchen door which opened onto the small rear verandah. It was the sound of subdued giggling, then a torrent of words, vaguely familiar but totally incomprehensible, which made her look round enquiringly. A young man stood in the open doorway, showing his large white teeth in a wide grin and gesturing towards the wicker basket which lay at his feet.

Like all the islanders she had so far seen the boy was dark-skinned, with slanting eyes and a mop of straight black hair, a typical amalgam of Chinese and Malay with enough Eskimo thrown in to prove that there had been comings and goings across the vast oceans in the distant past. When the boy realised she had seen him he transferred his attention, speaking in a kind of pidgin English which had Deena looking in wide-eyed admiration.

'Good day, Missy. Bad day go.' He waved a casual hand to the open door. 'Bad wind go. This day good, Missy.'

'Yes,' she agreed. 'Bad day go.' And she repeated his dismissive gesture. 'You have eggs? Bananas?' She indicated the basket lying beside his broad bare feet.

'Big fishee, Missy. You like?'

'Fishee?' she enquired cautiously.

'Sure. Sure.' And to prove his point he bent down, lifted the lid from the basket and drew out something black, wriggling furiously as it tried to escape the strong fingers gripping it below the head. 'Big fishee, Missy.' He looked in amusement at the eel's unavailing efforts to free itself.

'You kill?' To emphasise her meaning Carla brought one finger across her throat in a meaningful gesture.

'Sure. Sure.' He nodded amiably, then said something Carla couldn't understand, but the way he held up three fingers told her he was negotiating a price. She shrugged doubtfully. As she had nothing but Hong Kong dollars in the handbag which had been rescued from the plane she was uncertain what to do, but she went to collect it in any event.

The three dollars which she held up to his astonished gaze were evidently much more than he had been asking, but he swiftly, with a triumphant glance at the admiring Deena, pushed them away in a pocket of the velvet bolero which he wore on top of his sarong. Then, coming further into the kitchen, he said something, Deena handed him a large knife and with one quick move he removed the eel's head.

Carla, who had always been a bit squeamish about blood, averted her head and tried to close her ears to the nervous flapping from the sink.

'Please, can you take the skin off too.'

For a moment he looked at her uncomprehendingly but she went through the actions of peeling a banana which he understood and turned to pick up the knife again. He had almost finished when Carla heard a tiny exclamation and looked round to see the boy holding up his left hand, both he and Deena staring in dismay at the blood which spurted from the fleshy part of his thumb.

'Oh dear.' Carla frowned, and forgetting all about her nausea, she went to him and pressed the two sides of the jagged wound together, glancing up at the face that seemed to have grown suddenly pale and from whose features all signs of bravado had disappeared.

Half an hour later, just as she was finishing bandaging the wound, the kitchen door opened quite suddenly and Dr Gérard walked in. His swift glance took in the picture in a moment and Carla, after a startled look in his direction, completed her job, tied the ends of the bandage and snipped off the ends with the scissors.

'I'm sorry, I had to use one of your bandages. I found some sterilised packs in one of the drawers in the bedroom.'

'What happened?' The dark eyebrows were drawn together in a frown of concentration as he looked at Carla's pink cheeks, at the boy, then on to the skinned eel in a basin on the draining board. He addressed some questions to them in the local dialect and listened to the torrent of words that came from Deena and the boy.

'I think,' Carla turned away and began collecting the things she had used for the small operation, 'he could do with an anti-tetanus jab. If you have one.' She hadn't meant to be sarcastic.

'Yes, I agree with you.' When she swung round he was holding the boy's injured hand in his, frowning over the bandage, then with a sudden upward glance looked at her intently. 'I'll take him down to the surgery.'

When they had gone Carla continued with her preparations for the meal automatically, hardly remembering that she was supposed to be giving Deena some instruction, her fingers moving deftly as they sliced vegetables and cut the fish into small pieces. She knew she was disturbed by something and it was only when Marc came back that she began to realise what that something was.

She was relaxing in the sitting-room when he arrived

—she saw him from the corner of her eye, leaning against the door looking at her for a few moments before she put down the magazine, speaking without looking at him.

'How is he?'

'He's all right.' He levered himself from the wall and walked over to where she was sitting. 'He wasn't very keen on the needle, but then no-one is. Once it was over he thought it was nothing. A bit of a status symbol, in fact.'

Unexpectedly he sat down on the settee beside her, reaching out his hands to take hers. 'Your hands. How are they?' Instinctively she uncurled her fingers, watched the dark silky hair as he bent to scrutinise them.

'They're all right.' Her voice hardly shook. 'Much better.'

'And your bruise.' His hand moved to her forehead, sweeping back her hair.

'I told you,' her laugh was tremulous, 'none of my injuries was serious. I'm fine.'

'The shoulder and ankle,' he persisted. 'All right?'

'Perfectly.' There was a note of condescension, as if she found his belated attention a source of amusement. 'You were quite right when you said that a night's sleep would work a miracle. I've one or two aches, but nothing I wouldn't have had after a hard game of squash. And that salve you gave me for my hands is nothing short of magic.' Laughingly she examined her hands. 'It's so good that I put some on the boy's wound before I strapped him up.' Too late she wished she had considered her words before speaking.

'Ah yes.' With a lazy movement he got up and stood

there, looking down at her with an expression of spe-
culation. 'Ling's accident. I was just going to speak to
you about that.'

She felt her face grow warm, her pulse increase. 'Oh
yes.' She forced herself to reach out casually for the
magazine. 'I hope you didn't mind me suggesting anti-
tetanus. It seemed the obvious thing.' Her fingers riffled
the pages.

'Not at all.' His tone was mildness personified.
'Another opinion is always valuable.'

'Oh come.' She laughed and put her head back showing her white teeth. 'Or I'll think you're getting at
me.'

'No, I'm not. But I confess I'm rather puzzled. How, I
ask myself, how is it that Miss Carla Younger achieves
such a professional looking bandage?'

'Is that what you ask yourself?' No longer prepared to
suffer the disadvantage of him looking down at her she
rose with a languid move. 'Maybe that's because you've
brainwashed yourself into thinking that Carla Younger
is so utterly incompetent that you can't cope with the
idea that she can put on a simple bandage.'

'Only,' he grinned suddenly, 'this wasn't a simple
bandage. Every nurse will tell you that bandaging a
thumb is a most difficult and frustrating job. And yet,
you managed it with more expertise than I've seen in
many major teaching hospitals.'

'Oh, I'm flattered. All those first-aid classes have paid
off, after all.'

'Don't talk nonsense. I'm not blind. There was something very professional about the way you dealt with
that, in the way you spoke to me when I came in.' His

eyes narrowed. 'Are you going to tell me that you've no nursing experience.'

'I don't have to explain anything.' It was the old sense of failure that made her flare at him so angrily. 'Especially not to you, Dr Gérard.'

'That's true enough.' His laconic tone sounded like an insult. 'I've thought many things of you, Carla,' she wondered if he had chosen deliberately to use her Christian name, 'but I've never thought you were afraid to admit the truth. And I can only assume from your evasive answer that you did take up nursing at one time.'

'Assume what you like.' She paused. 'It seems that our whole relationship is based on your assumptions about me. Mostly wrong, as it happens.'

'So,' his raking glance continued to disparage, 'what happened? Did you find it too difficult? Too different from the kind of good life you were used to?'

Carla stared back at him, feeling the colour drain from her face. 'Something like that.' She stifled the sob rising in her throat. 'You must find it very satisfying to have all your prejudices confirmed. It wasn't quite as simple as you would like to make it. But you're right. I found I couldn't take it.'

'And you came running home to Daddy. Who no doubt would buy you a dozen new dresses to console you. How long did you stick it? A month? Six weeks?'

'Two and a half years, as it happens. I was at the Edinburgh Royal nearly two and a half years. I left just before I would have qualified for my SRN.'

'And you couldn't stick it just a few months longer?' His voice was as cold as ice.

'That's right.' She swallowed the lump in her throat. 'I

couldn't stick it any longer.' Wild horses wouldn't have dragged from her the real reason for her giving up her training, all her instincts now were to confirm him in his low opinion of her. 'And as you say, my father did his best to make it up to me. But,' she frowned as if it was difficult for her to remember, 'I think it was a diamond watch. Yes,' she felt a thrill of triumph when she saw his eyebrows come together, 'I've always had plenty of dresses! But what sticks in my throat, Doctor,' her voice hardened, eyes flashed with indignation, driving old regrets from her mind, 'is the way you keep throwing my father's money in my face. It is rather noticeable that you don't do it with him. And I have heard,' recollection of the odd snips of gossip came back to her, 'that your own family isn't exactly scratching a living.'

'I'm not against people with money.' His eyes moved over her face, showing total indifference to her passionate defence. 'It's only when people use their money to avoid all of life's problems. As for your father, I have the utmost respect for him. From what I understand *he* built up his business from nothing. All *he* has is a result of his own hard work. That I can admire. As far as my own family is concerned I can't deny what you have said. All I can claim is that I haven't made that an excuse for sitting back and doing nothing.'

'Bully for you,' Carla spoke nastily. 'How wonderful it must be to have such a high opinion of yourself. It must be a great comfort to you when you're sitting here alone. You can bask in the glow of your own admiration with plenty of simple natives around to reinforce the idea that you're some kind of deity. Oh I've met doctors like you before, Doctor! Maybe that's one of the reasons I didn't stick to nursing. I just couldn't take the picture of myself, acting the sycophant to all these ordinary men who somehow had got the idea that they were half-way between Superman and God. And now,' angrily she flung away from him, 'if you can bear to excuse me, I think I'll go and finish setting the table . . .'

'Well . . .' his voice was cool, as if all her angry words had scarcely registered, 'you might as well remove one of those places.'

'What . . . ?' She whirled round in time to see his gesture towards the table. 'What . . .' her eyes widened in sudden fear and she made no effort to control the trembling of her voice, '. . . do you mean?' Her mind was filled with the last sight of that cockleshell boat being tossed and dropped by the sea. Her attention was drawn from his face as he reached into the pocket of his shirt and he pulled out a piece of paper.

'No, Carla.' His voice was a shade softer than she was used to hearing. 'Colin's all right. I'm sorry, I didn't mean what you're thinking. He sent this note back with Teko. Something's gone wrong with the radio and they're staying to fix it. That's all. He's staying on Mainland overnight.'

'Staying the night.' As she repeated the words Carla felt waves of apprehension, perhaps even a little fear, wash over her and looking into that handsome face she saw a flash of some kind of emotion disturb that habitual remoteness. But the expression was so immediately hidden that she found it impossible to identify. Her attention was drawn to the piece of paper he was holding out to her. Automatically she reached to take it from him.

Dear Both,

Having a bit of trouble with the sender, but I'm sure I can get it going. There's a box of spares which should be useful but it will take time. I hope you can do without me for the night!! Be good.

Colin

As she read the final facetious words Carla felt the colour rise in her cheeks and, turning to hide her reaction, allowed the piece of paper to drop onto the cloth. The cutlery rattled with unnecessary vehemence as in sudden irrational anger against him she cleared his place noisily.

'He's so pig-headed,' the words flared from her.

'Why do you say that?' the voice behind her drawled.

'Because,' the green eyes were flashing as she whirled round to include him in her aggravation, 'because I've never known him to think of anyone but himself.' Even as she spoke she was silently apologising to Colin.

'I should have thought in this case he was thinking very much of you.'

'Of course he wasn't.' It would have been difficult to explain the sting of tears behind her eyes. 'Otherwise he would have come back instead of leaving me here . . .' She broke off just in time, but still regretting she had said as much.

There was a long silence when they stared at each other, Carla searching his face for some response, some indication of sympathy for what she had said. But there was none, just a steady quiet contemplation which told her nothing, then a swift turning away while he spoke to her over his shoulder.

'I've one or two things to do down at the surgery, then I must have a shower. I shouldn't be much longer than an hour.'

While she put the finishing touches to the meal Carla had plenty of time to contemplate her impetuosity in revealing so much of her feelings. It was the last thing she would have chosen to do with Marc Gérard, but, as always, when she was exposed to his disapproving cold manner, self-control was something she might never have learned.

Still, she drew in a deep breath as she put the rice in a warm bowl and the eel into the only other dish that was available, it was done now and there was no point in brooding. So long as she profited from the experience and didn't make the same mistake again. She put some of the food on a plate for Deena and left the rest where it would keep warm until they were ready to eat.

It was quite dark when Marc returned to find her in the sitting-room, lying back in one of the chairs, the long legs elegantly crossed, her hair immaculate, quite as if she were in the drawing-room at the Peak instead of in a tiny hut on a remote island. He stood for a moment in the doorway and although it had not been her intention, some weakness made Carla look up at him, noticing the still damp hair, the slight concession to formality in the fresh silk shirt, the red paisley-patterned tie. She swallowed some obstruction in her throat as she watched him walk, with that easy athletic stride, across the bare floor to the small wall cupboard.

'Drink?' His voice was as mild as if she were a welcome visitor in a normal situation, instead of someone he would have been more than happy to do without.

'No thank you.' Her voice was less crisp than she had intended as she realised, for the first time in her life, what it was to long for some artificial boost to her confidence.

'Go on.' He came to stand in front of her, looking down from his height and holding out a glass in her direction. He actually smiled down at her and to her dismay Carla felt her heart give a curious flop and begin to hammer loudly against her chest. Instinctively her fingers went out to close round the glass and it would have taken more control than she possessed to resist a responding smile. Briefly their fingers touched and a faint shock, as if she had flicked the live terminal on a car battery, ran up her arm. It was impossible to look elsewhere than into his eyes, impossible when he was looking at her so intently. His lips moved, the voice with the slight foreign accent sent a shiver down her spine, although his words were at that instant meaningless.

'You have made the point with me.'

'The point?' She raised the golden liquid to her lips.

'That you don't drink much. There's no need for you to go on proving it.'

She didn't reply. Indeed there was nothing to say. Instead she studied him over the rim of her glass, hoping her gaze was cool, determined to do nothing which might betray her feelings. Then, to her dismay, she found that he was looking at some tiny marks on her hand, that he was bending down to look at them.

'You have cut your hands again.'

Knowing that her slim fingers had never looked worse, she curled them round in an attempt to hide the chipping nail varnish, then with a laugh rose, sliding away from the chair to avoid contact with him.

'It's nothing. Only,' with an attempt at calmness she put her glass on the table and turned towards the kitchen, 'when you have time perhaps you could sharpen some of your kitchen knives. Cutting an eel into bite-sized pieces is the most frustrating thing when you have nothing but a blunt knife. But now I must get the meal . . .' And with a breathless rush she escaped.

'It's good.' His approval when he tasted the dish made Carla feel giddy and light-hearted. 'I hope you showed Deena how to do it.' He grinned and once again, just when she was deciding that the earlier surge of emotion had more to do with an empty stomach than with Cupid, her heart performed that curious somersault.

'She was there when I did it.' Her eyes shone with the sudden unexpected surge of happiness. 'But to be honest, I don't know if I could repeat it myself. I simply put in what I could from your now empty tins.' Recklessly she raised to her mouth the glass of wine he had poured. 'A few shreds of ginger, lots of onion finely chopped and garlic, of course.'

'Well, it's delicious.' He prodded a piece of the flesh with his fork. 'I hadn't realised how good eel could be. But I must confess—again—I'm surprised to find you such a good cook.' The mildness of his expression changed to one of searching intensity. 'As well,' he added enigmatically.

'As well as what?' Something in his expression made Carla counter sharply. 'I got the distinct impression that you thought I was particularly helpless. "A spoiled little idiot," I think that was one of your descriptions.' Even as all the pain of his contempt returned to wound her she was asking herself why she had to introduce this strident discordant note.

'Brat was the word I used.' His voice was calm and he showed no sign of being put out by her attack, but she was unwilling to give way to him.

'As well as what?' she insisted.

Marc put down his fork and sat back in his chair. Slowly, without taking his eyes from her face, he raised his glass. 'As well as being beautiful.'

Between them time seemed to stretch endlessly. Carla felt all the pain inside her ease and soften as she gave herself up to the bewildering sensation engendered by his words. It wasn't by any means the first time she had heard them and that made the perplexing weakness all the more difficult to cope with. Until she remembered just how much she had been hurt by this man and the sound of her chair being pushed back made an ugly screeching. 'I'd better get the next course.' And a moment later she had escaped to the security of the kitchen.

The rest of the meal was completed more or less in silence so that it came as a surprise to her when he said,

'How would you like to go to a party tonight?'

'A party?' The green eyes flicked up to look at him. 'What do you mean?'

'I mean a party.' He shrugged, then as if slightly self-conscious he rose, pushing back his chair and throwing down the napkin. 'In the village they are celebrating the passing of the storm. They take the opportunity at the slightest excuse. They expect me to go along. And tonight they have asked me to bring you as well.'

'And you?' In spite of herself the jeering note was back in her voice again. 'Have you been fighting an internal battle about it? To pass on the invitation or not?'

'I suppose so.' A flicker of a smile touched his lips so that her fascinated gaze moved to his mouth. 'We have such a rasping effect on each other that it did cross my mind to wonder if we were entirely compatible partners for a party.'

'Combatible or compatible?' she enquired sarcastically.

He shrugged again, the smile disappearing from his face. 'As you say. Anyway, I've passed on the invitation—it's up to you to make up your mind. I shan't influence you.'

'Well, if that's your attitude . . .' she began indignantly.

'Oh for God's sake . . .' he burst out angrily. 'I'm not in the mood to exert myself to be gallant to you.'

'That's nothing new,' she snapped. Then waited as the silence lengthened between them.

'Look, Miss Younger. This has been a difficult time for both of us. I've been stitching and strapping up minor wounds all day and there's nothing I feel more like doing than going to bed and sleeping. But these people are simple and if I don't go they will think they have offended me in some way. So I'm prepared to go along and put in an appearance at their celebration, thanksgiving, whatever you like to call it. Whether you care to do the same is up to you.' As he turned away Carla noticed the dark shadows beneath his eyes and it occurred to her to wonder just how much sleep he had had the previous night.

Nevertheless it wasn't easy for her to climb down and

to make it easier she turned away from his scrutinising expression and busied herself with collecting the dirty dishes. 'When are you leaving?' Her voice was as cold as she could make it.

'In about half an hour.'

'All right. Thank you for asking me.'

'Thank you for coming.' His voice was dry so that she had the absurd inclination to giggle. Fortunately she was able to control herself until she had reached the kitchen and could lean on the sink and laugh until the tears rolled down her cheeks.

CHAPTER SEVEN

THE path through the trees, along which Carla had previously wandered just a short way, followed the river for about five hundred yards, looped round the pool with the low waterfall where she knew Marc showered since she had arrived on the scene to disrupt his normal routine, then turned inland across the interior of the island.

A moon gleamed fitfully through the clouds as she followed him along the narrow road, the tops of the high palms swayed in the gentle breeze, scents of frangipane and hibiscus drenched the nostrils with their heady fragrance as he turned to offer her a hand to help her over a tree uprooted and tossed down by the storm.

'It seems strange . . .' She tried to escape from the emotion which his touch brought by talking in a matter-of-fact voice, but was defeated by the breathless way the words came from her lips. 'Strange that the hospital and your bungalow are so far from the village.'

'Yes.' They paused for a moment on the central peak which was no more than a raised piece of ground, scarcely affording a view above the tree tops. 'But as I told you, it's simply that the Japanese built the bungalow so they could keep an eye on the southern approach to the group. They cleared all the trees in front of the buildings where it's now so overgrown. It was easier simply to use what was there than try to make a suitable house. Even though it leaves a great deal to be desired it is comfortable enough for the time that my researches will last.' After what seemed an eternity he released her hand and together they walked along the winding path. 'The hospital was easy enough to build with local labour and it gives me all the facilities I need. Emergencies are few and far between. Apart from stitching the odd wound and giving the occasional dose of antibiotic, modern medicine isn't much in demand. In spite of everything they're a fairly healthy people, apart from this one weakness.' As they came again to the flat ground he paused so they could hear the faint drift of music coming through the trees. 'Come on.' Suddenly he grabbed her hand, grinned at her, his teeth gleaming whitely in the moonlight. 'Try to forget for an hour or two just how much you dislike me. It's a party, let's enjoy ourselves.'

'I thought,' her mouth trembled as he swung her round to face him, 'I thought it was you who disliked me.'

'Did I say that?' With a swift disconcerting move he brushed the hair back from her forehead, cradled her face in his hands. 'Did I really say that?' It was to himself he spoke, wonderingly. As if he were wrestling with some insoluble problem. 'But we all say things we don't mean.' About them the high calamus rustled disturbingly in the warm sighing wind. 'And do them sometimes.' Then, without another word, his hands dropped to his side and he turned, leading her in the direction of the village.

It was like many simple settlements she had seen in the

more isolated corners of Malaya and on the hundreds of islands scattered across the South China Seas. At one time when she had accompanied Colin on many of his trips such places had been familiar enough, but it was a long time since she had seen a place quite so untouched by western civilisation as Dalaoa. The huts, mainly of attap but one or two roofed in corrugated iron, formed a rough circle about the square and it was easy to imagine that during the day stalls would be set up with whatever produce was available, fish, perhaps a few eggs, bananas and coconuts for sale or barter.

Several small streets led from the square and from one of these a large garishly-coloured dragon emerged and, to the accompaniment of ringing bells and crashing cymbals, made its way sinuously towards them. Red smoke spurted from his nostrils as he reared menacingly in front of them, refusing to go away until they had donated some gift to propitiate the evil spirits. Marc parted with a small packet of cigars, Carla some tubes of sweets which she had rescued from the plane and the beast, placated, lumbered away from them in search of further quarry

Then they were free to wander among the village folk, all of whom seemed to know Marc, although their glances at Carla were shy and curious.

They spent some time with Omar who appeared suddenly, insisting that they sit on chairs in front of his hut while he fetched gourds filled with some kind of coconut drink.

'It's lovely, Omar.' Carla found it surprisingly cool and refreshing.

'Yes, it's lovely.' Amiably he agreed with her. 'Very

lovely.' And he looked disappointed when she refused some more. Then he offered first to Carla then to Marc a wooden plate with a few tiny cakes.

Carla nibbled cautiously, knowing from past experience that the Chinese had the habit of adding onion to their sweetmeats, especially those made for some special celebration, but these had a delicious flavour reminiscent of honey and coconut and just a hint of nutmeg. But not a whiff of onion. When she complimented him he accepted her congratulations with grave courtesy.

When they left to continue their circuit of the village they had to edge into doorways as the dragon and the crowd about him surged past, Carla putting out a hand to accept the orchid offered by one of the bolder young men, but all the time conscious of the protective arm with which Marc pulled her out of the path. When the road was again silent and deserted they continued, Carla regretting the speed with which he dropped his arm from her waist, dismayed by the pain her regret caused. She tried to speak casually, longing for something to take her mind off her own restlessness.

'How much longer will you be here, Marc?'

'Two more months. And then . . .'

'And then?' she prompted when he appeared to relapse into a melancholy silence.

'And then I expect I shall go—'

But what he had been about to say she never heard, for from somewhere ahead of them, away from the fringes of the village which they had just reached, came a sound of such anguish that they both stopped abruptly, four eyes searching into the undergrowth for the source of the voice. For that it was a human voice was unmistakable and as they stood stock still it came again, a scream diminishing to a long agonising moan which faded to utter exhaustion. And then started again.

'Carla.' In the few seconds since they had heard the first sound Marc had thrown off the casual relaxed air, now he was the doctor, used to giving orders, to being obeyed. 'Go back to find Omar. Tell him to come at once. Have you got that?'

'Yes.' Anxiously she looked up at him. 'But you will wait till he comes, you won't try to go in there on your own?'

In the moonlight she saw a faint smile on his face. 'There's no danger. It's a woman in labour, that's all.'

'That's all?' There was indignation in her voice.

'Oh, don't be such a feminist.' There was a trace of impatience in his reply. 'It's a perfectly natural function and all she probably wants is a little assistance . . . Now go off like a good girl and find Omar.' And without waiting to see if she was going to do as she was told, he turned and strode away into the undergrowth.

It took less than five minutes for Carla to rush back and find the house where they had left Omar. The little square was empty, but from the other narrow street leading off she could hear all the sounds of continuing celebration. As she called Omar's name through the open archway she wondered briefly what she would do if he weren't inside, but almost at once he answered her call and appeared at the door, wiping his mouth in a way that told her he had been disturbed at his food. Briefly, simply, she told him what her message was and after turning inside for a moment he accompanied her to where she had last seen Marc.

Even as they reached the spot that long wailing cry rang out again, causing a shiver to run down Carla's spine. Then almost at once she heard Marc's voice engaged in some sort of argument with one or two men who seemed determined to misunderstand what he was saying.

'Missy. You wait.' Omar left her and went forward towards where she could now see a faint light shining from an open doorway.

She stood shivering slightly in spite of the heat of the night, listening while the conversation, now with Omar clearly acting as interpreter, continued in a more placid vein but interrupted by the sounds of pain which had by now settled to an almost continuous moan. At last she heard Marc say with ill-concealed impatience,

'Well, tell them, Omar, that it's impossible. Their way we shall lose both of them. The mother and the child.'

She held her breath while Omar in rapid excited language explained to the unseen listeners, then a silence while the ultimatum was considered. A particularly loud sobbing cry came from the woman inside the hut, appearing to make them come to a speedy decision. She heard a single word uttered and then Marc came hurrying through the jungle towards her.

'Carla. Go back to the hospital.' A thought seemed to occur to him. 'You can find your way?'

'Yes. I . . . I think so.'

'Just remember when you come to that uprooted palm, you remember the one we spoke about on the way over, remember to keep right and then straight on.'

'Yes. I know.' It was difficult to inject some confidence into her voice when she felt so little.

'Good.' It was amazing how such an everyday word spoken with only modest approval could make her heart soar in this wild manner. 'Then when you reach the hospital you'll find a small steriliser next to the sink. Fill it half full and switch it on. But first you'll have to start the generator. Do you think you can manage that?' And without waiting for confirmation, 'It's easy enough. Just go outside to the shed and turn the wheel as quickly as you can till you hear the engine fire. We'll need some boiling water, but I'd rather have a little that's really boiling than a lot just hot, so don't put too much in. Then you could go up to the bungalow and put on a kettle to be on the safe side.'

'All right.'

'I don't want to leave the girl and Omar will have to stay to keep up the pressure on the husband and his brothers. They don't like the idea of a man having to look after her and they might change their minds. Even now I don't know if we'll be in time.'

'But what . . .' She felt fear clutch at her. 'What if you can't save her. What will they do?'

He shrugged then a reluctant grin crossed his face. 'Don't think about that now. I think we have a chance. And we'll bring her across as soon as we can rig up a stretcher of some kind. Remember your training. Remember I'm depending on you.'

She smiled at him. 'Then I'll go.' And without waiting any longer she turned and walked swiftly back to the square. There was no-one about as she crossed, although the noise echoed in her ears as she climbed the hill in the centre of the island and when she turned to look back, pausing to catch her breath, she could see the flickering lights outlining the crowds back in the square.

By the time she reached the tree where the path forked, sweat was pouring down her face and her knees were trembling with exhaustion. Still she forced herself on, knowing that if she failed in this she would have to face the scorn on Marc Gérard's face and the very idea made all feelings of fatigue evaporate.

She was breathless when she reached the compound, but she didn't pause as she went across to the small shed which she knew held the machine which generated electricity from oil. The batteries were capable of storing sufficient to provide lighting, inadequate as it appeared to be, but she was grateful enough to switch on the light so that she could see to swing the starting handle.

At first she thought that she would not be able to turn it quickly enough for the engine to fire, but she gritted her teeth and tried again, relaxing with a feeling of triumph when she felt it leap into noisy life. A moment later she was in the small operating theatre following Marc's instructions, half-filling the old-fashioned steriliser, seeing with relief the small red warning light come on before she turned to climb towards the house.

There in addition to the kettle she also filled a pot with water, lit both burners and collapsed into a chair. She had not meant to doze off, but that is exactly what she must have done for the next thing she remembered was a loud hammering on the door and then Omar standing looking down at her with a worried expression.

'Doctor say you come, Missy. Now.'

Of course. The water. She remembered, jumped up and ran to the kitchen, relieved that she didn't find it full of steam. Nevertheless both the kettle and pot were gently simmering. She snatched one and, turning to Omar who had followed her, pointed to the other.

'I've been waiting for it to boil,' she explained unnecessarily as they hurried down the path.

'Sure, Missy.' Relief was in his voice as he followed her through the clearing down to the group of medical buildings now gleaming with lights where all had been in darkness such a short time before.

She had to push her way through the small crowd of men standing outside the main hut, interrupting their chatter for an instant as they allowed her to pass through. Inside the door stood two women, fascinated and a little apprehensive as they stared at the figure lying under the searching brightness of the lights, a figure now ominously quiet, curiously draped in a sheet.

'Carla.' The man dressed in green theatre clothes turned from the side table where he was inspecting instruments, waving briefly at a pile of similar garments. 'Get into those and scrub up.' He returned his attention to what he was doing, dropping the gleaming tools into the steriliser while Carla was still staring at him as if he had gone mad.

'What . . . what do you mean?' The long-ago but still frighteningly familiar panic mounted inside her.

There was a long pause while he counted, then briefly, 'I need your help.'

'But I . . .' It was so ridiculous that she almost laughed. 'I can't help.'

'Why?' Above the mask his eyes were cold and raking.

'I just can't. I just know . . . I can't. Please Marc. Believe me I can't help.'

'You'll have to. I can't depend on any of those.' He jerked a head in the direction of the women looking at them from the door. 'They've almost killed her as it is.'

'But what . . .' She glanced at the still figure on the table. 'What are you going to do?'

'I'll have to perform a Caesarian. She'll never be able to give birth on her own.'

'I . . .' She tried to force firmness into her voice. 'I've no midwifery experience. Can't Omar . . . ?'

'No.' His interruption held a note of almost brutal satisfaction. 'It's bad enough for them to have to depend on a man. But me, a foreigner they can just about tolerate. They would never consider allowing a man who wasn't one of the family to have anything to do with it.' He pulled at the mask and bared his teeth. Certainly it could never have been called a smile. 'So you see, I have no choice. If I had, do you imagine I would have chosen you.'

'No,' she said and her voice was cold with despair. 'No, I don't imagine that.' And without another word she began to pull on the crumpled theatre garments he had indicated earlier, then crossed to where she could scrub her hands as she had been so peremptorily advised to do. As she did her eyes fell on the face of the patient and she could not prevent the protest that came to her lips. 'But she's just a girl.' Her accusation was for mankind in general and for him in particular.

'Yes.' Grim eyes looked into flashing green ones. 'Twelve. Thirteen at the most. Her pelvic girdle is so narrow . . .' He shrugged then, as if accepting her condemnation. 'Put on your cap and mask *before* you scrub up, Miss Younger.' And stood watching impatiently as she pushed her hair inside the green cap with savage little gestures.

Although it was all over in three or four minutes, at the time it seemed to Carla to be in slow motion. She watched his hands, sure and sleek in tight rubber gloves, move slowly towards the swollen stomach, yellow now with disinfectant and with a short dark line drawn where the incision should be made. When she saw the point of the gleaming scalpel press into the taut skin, bile rose in her throat as blood spurted. Only Marc's voice, imperative but unhurried, forced the vertigo from her brain so that she was able to lean forward with a swab held in a steady hand giving some pretence of efficiency.

'Wipe the blood.'

'Wipe her face.'

'Scissors please.'

Even his voice was slow, like a disc being played at half-speed, but there was something so reassuring about it that soon she forgot her own feelings in concern for the child-mother. Her eyes were able to return to the open line on the abdomen, to watch with grudging admiration the sure deft movements which cut deep into the layers of tissue. And her own automatic responses became calm and efficient.

Then quite suddenly the action moved into top gear, everything happening at such high speed that Carla had time to feel nothing but the excitement and wonder at the miracle of life. A tiny bluish form, inert and covered with a slippery bloody residue was eased from the small aperture by one gentle linked finger, pulled out then placed on his mother's stomach while a few movements separated his physical existence from hers.

Swiftly the tiny mouth was wiped with a damp swab then the infant was suspended by the heels and given a smart slap on the buttocks. At first there was no reaction, but while they both watched, Carla holding her breath, a faint shudder, then a surprisingly strident cry filled the small lungs. Without looking round she sensed the stir of excitement behind her, but she had no time to do more than notice it because the infant was thrust at her without ceremony.

'Here. Clean him up. There's cotton wool and cleansing oil in the cupboard next to the steriliser.' Beneath the mask she saw his mouth curve in a grin. 'As you'll have noticed, it's a boy.'

Behind her the two women moved impatiently again and Marc looked across at them. 'It's a boy,' he repeated, then said something in their own dialect. At once there was an excited jabbering which diminished slightly as they went outside to spread the good news to the men, but Carla scarcely noticed except to feel a surge of indignation that the sex of the baby seemed of more importance than the girl lying on the table.

But soon she was absorbed in the task of wiping the tiny body, then looking round to see if there was anything suitable for wrapping him in. She was trying to tear up some old soft sheeting into smaller pieces when she saw Marc gently slapping the girl's cheeks. Then one thin dark childish arm came up from the table in a faint ineffective gesture, as if trying to brush off an annoying insect.

'Good girl.' Unaware of Carla's interest Marc smiled down at the semi-conscious girl, brushed back with a soft hand a lock of damp black hair. 'That's right, *liebling*.'

'Is she going to be all right?' As she spoke, Carla wrapped the crying baby in a folded square of cloth then looked down at the dark indignant features in the crook of her arm.

'Yes.' There was a strange note in his voice that brought her head up to face him again. 'Yes, I think she'll be all right.' He smiled faintly and touched the now covered wound briefly. 'Except for a sore stomach she'll be all right.'

'Until the next time.' She spoke with a return of her indignation.

'As you say, till the next time.' He sighed. 'But I'll give old Amri a talking to and perhaps now that he has a son he'll leave her alone for a bit. He has three other wives, so . . .'

'Three others?'

'Yes. Of course you know how some of these people arrange their lives.' He spoke impatiently now. 'And on the whole it works well enough. It's perfectly natural to the men and the women. But,' he returned his attention to his patient, 'it's when young girls are involved that I find it so . . . so unacceptable.' He looked towards the door as one of the old women called across to the doctor and Omar poked his head inside the doorway to add to her plea.

'Doctor, sir. Please can Amri see his son?'

'Yes. All right.' He jerked his head in the direction of the door. 'Take the baby over.' He grinned suddenly. 'And they'll want proof that the baby is a boy. They won't simply take your word. Or even mine.'

Without answering Carla walked over to the door, standing just inside and pulling the shawl down from the baby's face. The women looked appreciatively at the wrinkled features, then stood aside as the men peered to look at the baby. Carla stared in dismay at the men whom she hadn't really noticed before, then she turned to Omar who was hovering in the background with as much interest as the others.

'Which is the father, Omar?'

'Here, missy.' Omar put his hand on the shoulder of the thin, ancient looking man. 'Here is Amri.' Then he launched into a torrent of words which were impossible to understand but which seemed to please the old man. Then when she had removed the cover so that the baby could be examined closely, Carla was allowed to return to the theatre.

She rocked the squalling infant, touching the petal soft cheek with a finger and at once the small head turned, the mouth searching instinctively for food, closed over it.

'Poor little chap, he's hungry.' The voice from behind her made her turn round and at once the expression in Marc's eyes brought the colour into her face. Just then the infant, realising his mistake, loosened his grip and opened his mouth again in a howl of protest and turned his head to nuzzle against Carla's breast. She felt her colour deepen, especially when Marc's hand came out to touch the child.

'Isn't he beautiful.' Her voice was shaky and tears threatened. 'But he's so hungry. And angry.' Once again she put out a finger, felt it gripped in his mouth, the powerful action of his gums and tongue evoking a strange trembling response which was unlike anything she had ever experienced.

'Give him to me, Carla.' Even Marc sounded strange. As if he too were disturbed by the unexpectedly emotional situation they found themselves in. 'I'll take him to the women. They'll find him something to eat and the mother will have a better night's sleep without him.' He walked across to the door, handed the baby over with instructions about how he was to be cared for, then he was back in the theatre looking down at her. There was a smile on his lips that seemed to reach his eyes. His hand came up and pulled the tight green cap from her hair.

'Thank you for helping me. I couldn't have managed without you.' His hand brushed against her cheek.

And the words, the way he spoke them, were so sweet that Carla, quite unlike herself and more resembling the maiden in a Victorian novel, felt she could have swooned with pleasure.

CHAPTER EIGHT

An hour later Carla was walking wearily back to the bungalow. She had washed the young mother, then had helped her to take some of the milky food made from a tin of powder in one of the kitchen cupboards. The girl had smiled wanly and had only just stayed awake until the last drop of the rich fluid had been drained from the cup. Then with a sigh she had lain back against the white pillow and a moment later she was asleep. Carla stood looking down at the thin childish face, at the dark shadows beneath the eyes, before with a sigh moving away, switching off the low-power light then taking the cup along to the kitchen.

When she had washed it and tidied away the things she had used she went back to the theatre where Marc and Omar were just finishing clearing up. She stood just outside the circle of light watching, until suddenly Marc raised his head to look at her.

'Can I do anything to help?' It was an effort to wrench her eyes from his and walk forward casually as she asked her question.

'No.' It was a long time before he answered. 'You've had a long night, Carla. You should go back to bed. I'm just going to write one or two notes and then I'll be up too.'

But when she reached the bungalow she found that

the fatigue which had assaulted her earlier had totally disappeared. Instead of going to her room to prepare for bed, she went through to the kitchen and put on the kettle to make some instant coffee, then she walked out to the verandah, leaning against the rail and looking up at the moon sailing high now in a sky that was the colour of pale silvery blue velvet. Against the background the trees were still and spiky black, like cut-out shapes in a child's book, sharp and clear.

Carla sighed, but it was a sound of wistful pleasure. In spite of the tortured, the impossible tortured relationship she had had with him, there had been something unexpectedly satisfying in that brief period back there in the hospital with Marc Gérard. He had been his usual gritty abrasive self. She would never expect, never even want him to be anything else. But underneath there had been a faint acknowledgement that she had performed better than he expected. He had almost said so. Grudgingly of course. A wry smile chased over the moonlit features. It was a strange sensation for Miss Carla Younger. She was honest enough to laugh at herself, to admit that all her life she had basked in her father's position, had enjoyed being the pampered adored only child of one of the richest men in the Colony. But now, all that had faded to insignificance. It meant much more to her to have the faint approval of the most aggravating, disapproving man she had ever met. She heard a step behind her and swung round, glad that the dimness hid from his probing, discerning eyes the blush that spread over her face.

'Still up?' He stood a yard away from her, the planes of his face shadowy and mysterious in the moonlight. 'I thought you would be so tired that you would be ready to tumble into bed.'

'No. I . . . I . . .' she stammered. The self-assured Miss Younger lost for words. Then, with an effort, 'I found I wasn't tired after all.'

'No. It's often like that after a birth. There's a strange feeling of exhilaration, no matter how often you are involved you never quite get used to it.' He sighed, a faint satisfied sound, then went forward to the rail, leaning against it while he continued to look at her. 'I'm sorry you had to be involved, but there was no help for it.'

'I'm glad I could,' she said primly. 'And the baby? Do you think he'll be all right?'

'I hope he will.' He sighed. 'I hope so. The old women have taken him to a wet nurse. If they can keep him with her for a day or two it will give his own mother a chance to recover.'

Now it was her turn to sigh as she turned from the dominating look in his eyes. She was very conscious of him standing there, so close to her, seeing with her the beauty of the romantic moon-washed world. 'I just feel so sad . . .' She shivered. 'That young girl married to such an old man.'

'Perhaps she doesn't mind. Has that occurred to you?'

'Yes, of course it has. But I don't believe it.' She slid a sardonic glance in his direction. 'Do you?'

'These people,' and to her ears he sounded irritatingly calm and undisturbed, 'don't have the same outlike as Western people. Who are we to say they should adopt our views?'

'I'm not saying they should. But I still can't believe

that a girl of thirteen is going to embark happily on a marriage with a man old enough to be her grandfather. Whatever her culture.' She laughed briefly. 'It's simply against human nature.'

'Perhaps some of our own present-day trends deprive us of any right to criticise other cultures.'

'Then,' conscious of rising irritation she was careful to speak sweetly, 'you don't see anything wrong in . . .'

'Carla.' His use of her name brought a shiver to her spine and it was impossible for her to resist the dark eyes. 'You know I dislike it. I said as much when we were down there.' He jerked his head in the direction of the hospital. 'But really I'm too weary to go on arguing with you.' He shrugged with an amusing mournful expression. 'It's all we ever do.' Unexpectedly his hand came out to smooth back from her face a curling tendril of hair. 'Why . . .' His voice deepened. 'Why do you suppose that is, *meine Schätze?*'

'What . . . what did you say . . . ?' So confused, so overwhelmed was she by his touch, by the bewildering softness of his voice, that she could understand nothing of what he had said.

'I said, or rather I asked why it was that we always seemed to . . . to waste our time by arguing so much?'

'I don't know.' Her heart was beating so loudly that she imagined he must hear it. She was unable to take her eyes from his face, from that strong mobile mouth. 'I . . . imagine it's because you disapprove of me so much.'

The silence between them lengthened, but his hand lingered still about the softness of her neck. 'Do you believe that?' he asked at last.

Carla did not answer. In fact she was unable to

answer, weakened as she was by the dominating possession of his eyes. At last, with a tiny shrug, he dropped his
hand to his side, turning away to lean again against the
rail while his eyes scanned the fresco of dark trees
against the sky. 'Go to bed, Carla. It has been a long day.
And with luck you will be travelling back to Hong Kong
tomorrow. I don't suppose,' and a trace of his old
sarcastic tone had returned to his voice, 'I don't suppose
your father relishes the idea of his daughter being
marooned on a desert island. Not at all the kind of thing
for Miss Carla Younger.'

'You asked why we were always arguing.' Her voice
was flat and hopeless. 'My theory is that you have such
an outsize chip on your shoulder, such a pathological
prejudice against women who are financially indepen-
dent, that as far as I'm concerned you just can't see
straight. Because I'm the daughter of a rich man, because I don't have a job and probably most of all,' her
laugh had a hint of hysteria, 'because I'm not a nurse.'
Making a supreme effort she regained some control,
although her voice shook slightly. 'There's no use discussing the matter any further. Goodnight.' She walked
towards the door.

'Goodnight.' His voice was as soft now as hers had
been abrasive, with a strong undercurrent of sadness
which she tried to ignore.

For a long time she leaned against the closed door of
her room wishing her heart would still its insistent
excited throbbing. One hand was pressed against the silk
of her blouse as if sheer physical force would control it,
but when there was no result she walked forward and sat
on the edge of the bed. Deep down inside her was the

certainty that only in tears would she find relief from the pain which seemed to have reached into every vestige of her being. But she had never been the weeping kind. Hardly since her mother's death had she given way to the indulgence of crying. And she had no intention of giving in now simply because a man like Marc Gérard delighted in rubbing her up the wrong way.

Slowly, calmly, she began to take off her clothes, folding them carefully, trying to find a balm in the unimportant minutiae of the everyday task. Then when she pulled on Marc Gérard's pyjamas she crossed to the mirror to comb her hair. She did it savagely, as if she were exerting some terrible revenge upon a bitter opponent. Only then did she turn off the light and slip between the cool sheets. It was true enough what he had said. It had been a long day. Perhaps if she were lucky tomorrow would see the end of this nightmare.

But sleep, necessary and overdue as it might be, was elusive. Carla lay for a while fighting the hopelessness that threatened her, trying to cultivate a calm that would bring the healing oblivion of sleep. But she had been lying in the dark for ages when quite suddenly she remembered something and sat up straight on the bed. She remembered putting a kettle on to boil. And she knew that she had not put out the light of the stove. Now, unless she wanted to be responsible for burning the bungalow to the ground . . .

A moment later she was padding across the floor in her bare feet. Cautiously she pulled open the bedroom door, relieved that the hinges made no sound to attract attention. The moonlight slanting through open shutters made the hall light as day as she ran swiftly across in the direction of the kitchen.

When she reached it she was relieved, annoyed with herself but still relieved that there was no light under the kettle. Either the light had blown out or someone had turned it off. A quick check of the position of the knob confirmed that the latter was the case and she felt a wave of irritation for Marc Gérard overtake her again. How wonderful always to be in the right she thought huffily as she turned to the door again.

She had just reached the door which led from the sitting room into the hall when a figure, large shadowy and quite unmistakable, barred her way. She was unable to hide the start of dismay that his unexpected appearance brought and a nervous hand closed the neck of the pyjama jacket she was wearing. They stood looking at each other in the room, unlit except by the moonlight.

'I . . .' she looked from his face to the glass in his hand, 'I remembered suddenly that I had left a light under the kettle.'

The dark eyes gazed at her without answering.

'I thought,' her laugh betrayed her nervousness, 'I'd best get up to see.'

'And what did you find?'

'I found that you had already turned it off.'

'Did you? How strange.' She sensed rather than saw the raised eyebrows, the cynical expression as his eyes flicked over her scantily clad figure. 'And if I said that I didn't turn it off what would you say then, Miss Younger? What excuse would you concoct then for trailing about the house in the early hours of the morning . . . ?' He paused and raising the glass to his lips drained it, setting it down carefully on a table just inside the door.

For a moment she stared at him, unable to understand his meaning, then as the enormity of it struck her she felt the colour burn in her cheeks. She struggled for calm and felt rather pleased with herself at the lightness of the tone she achieved.

'What you're suggesting is too ridiculous, Dr Gérard. I can only assume that what you've been drinking has fuddled your brain. But now I want to go back to bed, so if you'll let me pass . . .'

'I don't think that a glass of Coke is likely to have the effect you mention, Miss Younger.' His voice seemed deliberately condescending and offensive. 'I remembered I had put some tins of Coke out in the stream over a week ago and suddenly felt thirsty.' He bowed sarcastically. 'I'm explaining simply to clarify matters, not because I feel I have to justify my actions to you.'

Carla laughed nervously after a moment. 'Then what you suggest must seem doubly ridiculous, Doctor.' She was conscious of the hammering of her pulse in her ears and wet her lips.

'What was I suggesting, Carla?' His hand came out as it had done earlier when they had been standing on the verandah together. 'Tell me!' His voice was soft and beguiling, irresistible.

'That,' in spite of herself she was trembling, her voice and her body, 'that I had come out to . . . For some reason . . . I don't know.'

'Was it perhaps . . .' As he spoke his hand slipped from her neck down her arm to her fingers where it rested, casually enclosing hers. 'Perhaps that you could not sleep. That you were restless. That I was filling your thoughts,' he paused for a long time his eyes glittering at her in the dark shadow of the door. 'As you fill mine,' he finished with a faint smile that was no longer mocking.

'No,' she protested as she felt herself drawn towards him. 'No,' she said as his mouth brushed tantalisingly against hers. And then she was still, held immovably against that long hard body, all the aching sorrow melting away as his mouth took possession of hers. For just a moment she resisted, her lips pressed close together in an effort that exhausted her energy. And then it was bliss to relax, to soften against the tautness of him, to surrender to all those emotions which she had tried to ignore for so long.

Fire seared through her veins as she allowed his demanding searching lips to part hers, to explore her mouth with sensual tender force. A tiny moan signalled her total subjugation as she reached up to link her hands in the dark springy hair. His hands burned through the thin material she was wearing and when he spoke her name his voice was hoarse.

'Carla. Carla.' All trace of animosity had gone, replaced by an echo of her own wordless longings. She lay for a moment against his chest, her mouth touching the dark throat, hearing the loud strong beating of his heart. Her hands moved across his chest, rejoicing in the firm warm skin beneath her fingers.

Suddenly he groaned, catching her hands in his, taking them to his mouth, kissing the tips of her fingers and an instant later he had swept her into his arms and was striding across the hall to the open bedroom door.

He put her down by the side of the bed but still holding her in the circle of his arms about her waist, looking down at her, his possessive eyes refusing her any escape, even if she had wanted it. She continued to stare up at him, her eyes wide, green and wide and shadowy with emotion, the hair tumbled, the mouth soft and vulnerable.

And she saw the man who had always been cold and self-contained, his chest moving quickly as his hands tightened about her, pulling her more strongly to him. Instinctively her hand moved again towards his throat, slipping under the white shirt to lie on the warm skin above the hammering of his heart.

He smiled and frowned, imprisoning her hand with one of his before his mouth came insistently towards hers again. For Carla there was no question now. It had all been leading to this tempest of emotion between her and this man. All the searching, all the yearning was over. There was no way she could resist. No way she wanted to.

As his hand slipped over her shoulder, pushing the too large garment aside, she shuddered, but it was a reaction of sheerest pleasure. And when he moved to her breast, touching her with delicate sensitive fingers, bringing her senses to a quivering trembling crescendo, she allowed the tempest to envelop her.

Heart beat against heart with a wonderful rhythmic pulse, she arched her body to his glorying in the possessive hand determined to mould her against him. And then she was lying on the bed, the pyjama jacket tossed carelessly on the floor and she was cradling his head against her breast, leaning back in exultation as his mouth caressed her body. Her fingers twisted in his hair, imprisoning his intimate exploration.

But suddenly she heard him mutter some words as he wrenched himself away from her and before she had time to think, to understand what was happening, she was alone on the bed and the door had banged with quite exceptional savagery. A tiny moaning sob escaped her lips when she realised she was alone.

She had no idea how long she lay there as shock following upon shock quivered through her body, now trying to adjust to the sudden separation from his presence. Tears forced themselves beneath her closed eyelids, she felt them running down her cheeks into her hair, wetting the pillow. Then with a desperate gesture she rolled over, pulling the sheet about her, burying her face as she tried to stifle her throbbing pulse.

At last she regained control, turned over and lay staring at the ceiling, her hands spread out at her sides in an expression of appeal. She would never forget the intoxicating touch of his body on hers, like silk against silk. Wonderingly, despairingly, she touched her throat where his mouth had lingered, caressing. Then with a strange unreal feeling of curiosity she dragged herself up from the bed and walked over to the small mirror hanging above the low chest of drawers, looking at the half-naked body milky white in the faint moonlight.

It was a very feminine shape with a slender waist and full firm breasts which now ached with the passion of his lips. She passed her hands over them as if in some way she could capture the imprint he had left there. Then another groaning sobbing sigh which she had no idea that she had uttered echoed through the room. How could she bear it. Oh God. She whirled away from her own mocking reflection. How could she bear it if . . .

She threw herself onto the bed, feverishly twisting one corner of the sheet. If he does not love me I cannot bear it, she told herself. I cannot bear it if he does not love me. All I want is for him to love me. She had said it at last. Admitted what she had known from that first glance across the gaming room at Macao. She loved him with all the foolish desperate ardour of a teenager. She loved a man who didn't even like her. He had told her so, shown her that he disliked her from the beginning. So much that his self-respect would not allow him to respond to the natural sexual attraction that had flared between them. Any other woman he would have made love to. But not her. Not Carla Younger.

I can't bear it, she told herself again, but now with a calm despair. I cannot bear it if he doesn't love me. But of course she knew that he didn't and so of course she must. And perhaps if the Fates were kind she would be off this island tomorrow. In fact she decided that even if Colin didn't come she would persuade one of the islanders to take her across to Mainland. For she could not stay here a moment longer.

It was dawn when at last she slept. Only when she had given up hope that she would ever be able to rest again, oblivion stole over her taking her off into a deep relaxing dreamless sleep. Then she woke and lay passive for a few moments before memory returned to strike her with a savagery that made her groan and close her eyes again.

But she could not lie escapist in the bed for ever. A glance at her watch confirmed that it was mid-morning and that if she were lucky she might possibly avoid meeting Marc for an hour or two. So using his towelling bathrobe she hurried out to the little lean-to at the back of the bungalow for a shower.

Deena was in the kitchen when she returned and had the kettle ready to make some coffee. She smiled amiably at Carla and nodded at the enquiry about the previous night's party.

'Has the doctor gone to the hospital?' Even for Deena's sake she tried to make her query casual.

'Oh doctor. Missy.' Deena pressed one hand apologetically to her mouth then grinning led the way through to the sitting-room and pointed to the envelope lying beside Carla's cup and saucer. She saw her name emblazoned in flowing black characters, picked it up, her heart hammering again in that particularly uncomfortable way.

'Thank you, Deena.' She turned away from the girl's curious eyes, waiting till she had returned to her bedroom before putting one long finger under the gummed flap. There was no greeting at the top of the letter, just a bald statement of his activities.

Today I have to go to a small settlement on the other side of the island and may be away all day. I'm sorry. [I bet, thought Carla.] It just occurred to me that you might care to have a swim. As the coasts are not safe you could use the pool under the waterfall. It is deep and clean and quite private.

            Yours,
            M. G.

When she had read it Carla didn't know whether to feel like laughing or crying, but in the end did neither.

She was pleased of course that she was spared the trouble of making conversation with him. And if by chance she was still here this evening, which heaven forfend, she would make some excuse so that they could eat separately. She would say that she wasn't feeling like food and would stay in her room. It would be easier for both of them like that.

In the meantime, she had the day to get through. Part of it she spent in washing her clothes, feeling thankful that the intense heat dried things very quickly. Then when she was wearing her own navy slacks and red blouse again she went down to the hospital and spent a little time with the girl who had been the central figure in the previous night's drama. Carla found her sitting up in the low charpoy surrounded by what seemed to be the entire female population of the village, apparently recovered from her ordeal, perhaps even enjoying the sensation she had created. Nevertheless, Carla thought as she turned away how very young and childish she still seemed in spite of the baby which she held to her breast. It was foolish to hope that she would avoid an immediate second pregnancy for it was rather unlikely that her husband would choose one of the older wives when he had the infinitely more attractive and apparently fertile young woman to share his bed. But still, she did hope that.

At lunch time, feeling singularly unlike eating, Carla contented herself with a glass of coconut milk and a small ripe durian, a fruit for which she had a passion. Then she lay on her bed for an hour, apparently reading from the paperback book she had found in the bedroom but in fact so obsessed with her own feelings that her brain seemed unable to absorb the written word. At last, in a gesture of despair and anger at her own foolishness, she threw the book into the furthest corner of the room, feeling pleased when it dropped out of sight behind a chair. She hoped that Marc Gérard would be anxious to find it when he was restored again to his own room and that he would be unable to satisfy that anxiety.

Carla rose and went across to the mirror, trying to pretend that she couldn't see the deep shadows beneath her eyes, that her expression of listless depression wasn't a symptom of her own deep unhappiness. But she sighed and as she turned away she caught sight of the note she had tossed down earlier. She read it for the twentieth time, trying to discern beneath the bald uncompromising words some hint, some clue that would give her a little hope. But there was none. She had known that before she read it and in anger she screwed it into a ball and tossed it over to join the book behind the chair.

Go for a swim. She smiled grimly. Take a shower. It will cool you down in more ways than one. And maybe there was something in that piece of advice. She thought of the inviting pool in the shelter of the fringe of trees and thinking of it suddenly longed to dive into the deep clear water.

A moment later she was following the path that led alongside the stream and then branched off into the undergrowth. As she drew near, the sound of dropping water tantalised so that she ran the last few yards, pushing aside the hanging tendrils of vine which drooped from the trees, tossing her towel down onto the grass.

It was cool on the mossy ledge hanging a mere yard over the pool and the drifting spray of the waterfall made it cooler still when she held her face up to it. She knelt down, leaning forward so she could see her own reflection on the surface, wavering a little from the ripples set up by the cataract. Then she sat back on her heels, looking round with pleasure at the way the palms leaned towards the water as if they too longed to catch a glimpse of themselves in the surface. At the far side, where the stream joined the pool the ground sloped down forming a tiny sandy beach, the water lapped temptingly.

Carla could resist no longer. She took off her clothes, folding them in a neat pile, putting her shoes on top and then diving in, a long pale streak cutting through the water, crawling back and forth across the pool as if engaged in some terrible fateful contest.

It was blissful. Only once or twice had she found the courage for nude bathing, but the sensation was one that had never been forgotten. Of course on such a crowded island as Hong Kong it was hardly ever possible and she had never been brave enough to join all the other exhibitionists on the Riviera. No, foolish as it was, she could only enjoy nude bathing if she was on her own, if she was absolutely certain that she would be undisturbed.

The cool water was like a benison on her limbs, stroking with a persuasive silky intimacy, easing her bruised and battered spirit. When she had tired of the intense determined crawl she lay on the surface, looking down at the floor of the pool through the crystal clear water, watching the long waving fronds, seeing the tiny multi-coloured fish darting in and out of the concealing lacy weeds.

She was treading water, trying to decide whether she

had had enough, piling her soaked hair on top of her head and squeezing out some of the water, when she became aware of a tall figure standing at the end of the path watching her, a grin on the familiar dark face, his arm still supported in a slightly grubby sling.

'Colin.' With a swift stroke, Carla reached a patch of water lilies at the furthest side of the pool. 'You brute,' she spluttered spitting out water. 'You swine. Standing there watching me. Of all the dirty tricks . . .'

'Take it easy.' Still grinning Colin walked down to the edge of the low shelf and crouched down, never taking his eyes from the girl trying to shelter under the rather sparse vegetation. 'I wasn't standing there watching you as you so unkindly put it. I thought you knew me better than that. No, I simply came through the trees and there you were. I was stunned into silence by the scene.'

'I bet.' Carla crossed her arms across her chest. 'And the trouble is that I do know you.'

'Now would I do a thing like that, honey?' Colin's expression was injured innocence.

'Of course you would.' Carla's tone was waspish.

'We . . . ell,' he shrugged. 'Would you have been more pleased if I hadn't even noticed that you were swimming in the nude? For God's sake, love, I'm not blind. And I'm not going to pretend that I don't enjoy the sight of a pretty girl just as much as the next man. You must know I'm a page-three bloke.'

'Yes. That I do know,' Carla spoke drily. 'Now, if you'd kindly turn your back I'll be able to get out and put my clothes on.'

'Here.' He bent down and offered his uninjured hand, giving an encouraging jerk of his head.

'No, thank you. Just do as I ask and turn away.'

'Come on, honey. I'm an old married man. Besides being old enough to be your father.'

'Yes. I know about men who are old enough to be girls' fathers,' said Carla cryptically.

'What?' Colin looked confused.

'Oh nothing,' she snapped. 'I'm getting cold, that's all.'

'Come on, love.' He turned round and picked up the towel which Carla had dropped at the side of the pool. 'I promise that I'll keep my eyes closed tight.'

'All right.' One powerful stroke took her over to where Colin, eyes screwed shut, was leaning over the pool with his arm extended. 'Now if you do open your eyes, I promise you that I'll pull you right into the water. Promise.'

'Sure. I promise.' His voice was serious. 'Don't worry, love.'

Carla grasped his hand and felt herself pulled out with a single powerful heave, her feet touched the ground and she bent down to pick up the towel with an embarrassed little giggle.

And then as she held the towel in front of her, using one corner to wipe the water from her face, she saw behind Colin the bushes move as Marc Gérard bent his head beneath the draped green vegetation. When he straightened up he froze, his eyes flicking over Carla's dripping figure, seeing Colin without even looking at him. Carla stood as if turned to stone, feeling the blood drain from her heart. And he was gone. With one swift movement he had parted the curtain of vines and disappeared. But not before he had given her a glance of such searing contempt that she thought she would faint.

'Okay.' Colin's voice was full of patient humour. 'Can I look now?'

'Oh, for heaven's sake, Colin,' she answered snappily. 'Don't let's make a big thing of this. As you say, you're an old married man.' And then to her dismay she burst into tears.

CHAPTER NINE

'WHAT'S the matter, honey?' As they walked back to the bungalow his arm came out to pull her against him. 'Don't tell me you found a serpent in paradise?'

'No.' It was a pathetic attempt at laughter. 'I'm sorry, Colly. Sorry for snapping at you like that.' Surreptitiously she wiped her eyes with a corner of the damp towel. 'I don't know what came over me. I suppose it's all a reaction. The accident and then feeling trapped here.'

'Well, I shouldn't have thought it was as bad as all that.' He looked about him. 'People in Europe would pay the earth for a holiday in a place like this. And with a handsome doctor thrown in.' He paused, waiting for her to say something and when she didn't went on thoughtfully, 'Or was that the trouble perhaps?'

'Of course not.' Now she answered quickly enough.

'Sure?' They had reached the clearing and he turned her towards him, tipping her chin upwards with one hand, studying her closely with his intense blue eyes. 'Sure?' he asked again, gently, tenderly.

'*Sure.*' She laughed, this time more convincingly. 'Absolutely.' Firmly she turned away from him, slipped her hand in his arm as they walked towards the bungalow. 'Not unless you mean that we rub each other up the wrong way. I annoy him and he does the same to me. It happened when we met in Hong Kong so it was bound to get worse when we were thrown together like this.'

'Well, they say that's how all the best love stories start.'

'But that's only in books. Look at you and Lin. I thought it was love at first sight for both of you.'

'Yes.' His voice was considering. 'But you're different, love. You never do things the straightforward easy way. Besides, you're a romantic. And I guess that maybe Marc Gérard's the same, for all his cool detached manner. He's deep, and intense.' Suddenly Colin grinned and pulled her round to look at him again. 'Get me. Quite the philosopher in my advancing years.' Then his face grew serious again. 'Only, there's nothing I would like more than to see you settled and happy, Carla. You need a man to keep you under control. And a man like . . . Well, anyway.' He smiled. 'If I start matchmaking that will really be the end. I'll be taking up crochet next. Come on. We'd better go up and see the man himself. Oh and by the way, honey, I brought you a visitor. Someone who's very anxious to see you. In fact two of . . .'

'A visitor?' Carla stared at him, the green eyes wide with surprise. Then quite suddenly her face lit up, the wide mouth smiled showing the perfect white teeth. 'Oh bless you, Colly.' Leaning forward she kissed him briefly on the mouth, then she turned and ran across the soft grass to the bungalow, the long blonde hair streaming wildly behind her. 'Daddy.' She burst open the door leading from the verandah then ran into the sitting-room, 'Oh, Dad.' And as Bob Younger's arms came round her she felt the tears pricking behind her eyes again.

'Now, Carla.' Even the undemonstrative Scotsman's

voice wasn't quite steady as he stroked the back of her still damp head. 'It's all over. Soon you'll be back in your own room at home. Joan and I have been so worried about you and . . .'

'Joan?' Carla withdrew a little and looked up into her father's face, glad that she hadn't allowed any of the threatening tears to fall. Vaguely when she had come into the room she had noticed the tall figure of Marc Gérard standing in the centre of the room. But what she hadn't seen was Joan Christison sitting on the sofa, just out of sight. But now she rose and came forward smiling.

'Carla. It's wonderful to see you.' She hesitated shyly, her arms first coming out then almost at once, as if unsure of her reception, dropping to her side.

It took Carla only a split second to make up her mind. Afterwards she wondered if it had been the observant silent figure watching with his intense dark gaze which had influenced her. She thought not, for the moment she had turned to Joan, putting her arms about her neck and kissing her on the cheek, she knew she had done what she wanted.

'Joan. Thank you for coming. It's the most wonderful surprise to see you and Dad.' She turned round to include her father in the welcoming words and the suffusion of happiness on his face made her long to cry again. Instead she smiled.

'But how on earth did you get here? I didn't hear a plane. Besides, the runway isn't fit for landing. I was up there yesterday and . . .'

'Oh, it was all too easy.' Bob waved a hand in the direction of his fiancée. 'It was Joan's idea really. A friend of hers lives in Manila and she knew that he would let us borrow his cruiser. So that's what we did. We flew down as soon as the storm was over after we got Colin's message. This morning we picked Colin up from Mainland and came over. The boat is anchored just outside the reef and we all came in on a small outboard launch.'

'It's all so easy.' Carla smiled at Joan. 'Amazing what you can do when you know the right people. And Colly . . .' she turned round to look at him in mock reproof, '. . . didn't say a word. Just came down to the pool and howked me out of the water.' Deliberately she glanced at Marc Gérard as she spoke, then back to her father with only very slightly heightened colour. 'It was only when we had almost reached the bungalow he told me that he hadn't come alone. Thank you, Colly.' She smiled round in his direction.

'Don't mention it, honey.' He seemed deliberately to misunderstand. 'I'll howk you out of the water any time you like.'

'But now,' her father looked at his watch, 'perhaps we should all be thinking of going back to the ship. I've asked Marc to come and join us for dinner, Carla. We're in no hurry and it would be nice to have him with us for the last night. Show him how much we appreciate what he's done for you.'

Carla felt the colour rise in her cheeks, then drain away as he spoke for the first time. 'There's no need for that, Bob. Carla will tell you how little I've done. I'm not sure I've been a very good host. And in many ways I'm the one who's indebted to her.'

'Nonsense, my dear fellow. Anyway we'd better make a move. We'll have to make two trips of it. So what about us going first then you and Colly can be ready for the next run.'

For a moment Carla thought that Marc was going to refuse the invitation, her eyes held his challengingly as if daring him to come and have dinner aboard the yacht. There was a clash of wills between them and when he looked away from her she felt a moment's panic, followed by relief and perhaps even triumph, when quietly he agreed to the plan that had been suggested.

And then the two of them were left alone for a moment while Bob and Joan followed Colin outside, he pointing in the direction of the runway where the damaged aircraft still hung half-way between earth and sky. His voice could be heard discussing with his employer the best means of salvaging both the plane and its cargo, but inside neither of them paid any attention to his plans. They stood looking at each other and it was Marc who spoke first.

'I'm sorry about tonight. I . . .'

'Yes, I'm sorry too.' Her voice was as brittle as it had ever been. 'I know how anxious you must be to see the last of me.'

'I was going to say it would have seemed ungracious to refuse the invitation. And . . .'

'And you don't like being ungracious,' she mocked, and had the doubtful satisfaction of seeing his mouth tighten.

'I wish you would stop interrupting. It's a bad habit you have.'

'One of many,' she interjected sardonically.

'On that at least we can agree.' He looked at her with positive dislike. 'But when I said I was sorry it was you I was thinking of, strange as that may seem to you. I imagine my presence will add little to your reunion with your father and . . .' He stopped speaking but not before Carla realised that he had been about to include Joan's name with her father's. She felt guilty colour run into her cheeks and turned abruptly away in an attempt to hide it. Since coming to Dalaoa she had avoided any mention of her father's forthcoming marriage, determined not to give Marc the satisfaction of saying I told you so.

'You needn't let it worry you,' she said ungraciously. 'Naturally my father would like to thank you for what you have done and . . .'

'And you?' It was his turn to be sarcastic.

'As I was about to say,' she finished coldly, 'And I am very grateful too of course.'

'It was a pleasure, Miss Younger.' She saw his teeth gleam whitely. 'I don't suppose I'm the first man to say that by any means.'

She was staring at him, feeling as if she had been struck a blow beneath the heart, wondering vaguely if her own face looked as ravaged as his suddenly did when Colin stuck his head into the room.

'Come on, you two.' His voice was almost coy as he glanced from one to the other. 'You don't have to take all day to say goodbye to each other. You are meeting again in an hour or two. Oh and by the way, Marc. Do you think I could get someone to help me unload some of the boxes from the plane. It seems crazy to leave them like that.'

And without waiting to hear Marc's answer Carla pushed past him and ran outside to where her father and Joan were waiting for her to join them.

It was wonderful to be back to a luxurious life again. As she lay in the hot scented water idly rubbing her sun-tanned arms with a tablet of rich pink soap, Carla assured herself that she was perfectly content. The first thing she had done when she arrived on board was to go into the bathroom attached to her cabin, throw handfuls of bath salts into the bath and turn on the hot tap. Then she had drenched her hair with conditioning cream, tied it up in a scarf and stepped into the bath. The clothes that she had been wearing since the crash were strewn about the bathroom floor and she meant, whenever she got dressed again, to throw them overboard in a glorious final gesture. It had been a great relief to find that Joan had brought two suitcases full of clothes and makeup from home and that before she presented herself for inspection again the real Carla Younger would be re-established.

And what was so wrong with enjoying luxury? She refused to feel guilty about it. She would be fooling herself and other people if she didn't confess that she found this bathroom more enjoyable than the tiny shower room at the back of the bungalow. And she would enjoy the meal tonight prepared for them by the galley stewards on board. And she didn't doubt that if *he* were being honest he would say the same. Not that she had any intention of asking him. In fact the one intention she had was to say only what was necessary to him tonight, then get back to Hong Kong and forget everything as soon as she possibly could. He had been like a thorn in her flesh for too long. And she wouldn't be happy until the thorn had been severely dealt with. She began to hum to herself, a determined little frown disfiguring the smooth forehead.

Five of them sat down to dinner about half past eight, in circumstances so different from the ones she had been used to for the last few days that Carla could scarcely believe it. In the middle of the dark shining round table was the flower arrangement which she had completed just before the launch bringing Marc and Colin from the island had arrived. It had been Joan's suggestion and Carla imagined that she was being humoured when she was asked.

'Would you care to do the flowers Carla? I've never been much good at it and I remember how lovely your arrangements always look at the villa.'

'Of course I'll do them.' Her smile was rueful. 'It's nice to think I can do something properly. I've come to the conclusion, Joan, that I'm a bit of a parasite.'

'What nonsense.' Joan's tone was firm. 'You do most things well. I know you can cook and . . .' She hesitated.

'There you are, you see.' Carla's laughter was genuinely amused this time. 'And what?'

'And lots of things. You're a first class driver and you run your father's house beautifully.'

'That's nothing.' Her amusement died down as quickly as it had risen. 'Anyone could run a house like ours. But I will do the flowers. What style do you prefer? Constance Spry or ikebana?'

'I don't mind. Now come and I'll show you where they are.' Joan led the way down the central gangway towards the galley and threw open a large refrigerated cupboard. 'There's plenty to choose from. Your father insisted on going to the flower market in Manila and buying whole armfuls of flowers. These roses . . .' she touched a cluster of rosebuds with a pink-tipped finger, '. . . were specially for you.'

'Oh . . .' Carla picked up the bunch of roses and hid her face in them, hoping that Joan would not notice the brightness of her eyes.

'Yes.' Joan turned and led the way into the dining room. 'He has been so worried the last few days, Carla. And I can't tell you how relieved he was when he knew you were with Marc Gérard. He told me that when he heard that he knew you would be all right.'

'Yes.' Carla picked up a silver rose bowl from the centre of the table. 'I was perfectly all right with Marc.' And her voice was flat and devoid of emotion.

But now sitting opposite Marc Gérard, leaning forward to smile at him, Carla felt that she was getting her own back in a way that previously she couldn't have imagined. She was exerting herself to be good company, to be charming in a way that she had found very effective in the past. It would give her a feeling of having scored against him in the end if she could see a glint of admiration in his eyes. She had even felt a thrill of pleasure when she had seen the pink dress, the one he had been so very rude about at their first meeting, hanging in the wardrobe of her cabin. She had shaken out the delicate folds with a feeling of triumph, had slipped into its silken smoothness with a frisson of excitement, a thrill of narcissism when she glimpsed her own reflection in the glass.

And the moment when she had met him on board, when he had turned with her father from the rail where they had been leaning, watching the moon hanging above the dark water, she had known that he remembered. That swift glance over the bare shoulders return-ing to her face with an expression designed to reveal nothing told her a great deal. And excitement rose inside her.

'To you, Carla.' Her father had raised the glass he held in his hand and Marc had no choice but to raise his as well. And even the mockery of his eyes was a source of great satisfaction to her.

She caught sight of Joan at one time glancing from Marc to her, then sending a knowing little glance at her father, but even that could not halt the indiscreet way she flirted with Marc across the table. She had not intended to behave in this way. The idea hadn't even crossed her mind. But now that she was into it she was enjoying herself thoroughly, couldn't understand why she hadn't behaved like this on Dalaoa instead of being so abrasive, so unfeminine. And she was rewarded by a glimpse once or twice of cold anger as he looked back at her. Now that the meal was over, he held a thin dark cheroot between his long fingers and looked at her through the smoke, eyes faintly narrowed as if she was some form of particularly obnoxious insect. But beneath all his apparent dislike she sensed something else, some-thing more vital and intoxicating, an emotion that seemed to charge the whole room with the force of electricity. She realised that Colin was saying something to her and dragged her eyes reluctantly away from Marc's.

'Sorry, love,' she was at her sweetest. 'I didn't quite hear.'

'I was just saying about the roses. Asking Joan who did them.'

'Oh, that was me. Didn't you realise what an artistic girl I am?' She put out a hand to touch the pink rosebuds nestling in glossy dark green leaves but wondering if Marc would notice the elegantly varnished fingernails, so much a contrast from yesterday's chipped neglected look.

'Yes I did.' Colin entered into the spirit of the thing. 'It's one of the things I've always known about you.'

'Thank you, Colly.' She made a mocking little bow. 'It's nice to know there's someone who doesn't think I'm entirely useless.'

'Of course you're not useless,' Joan laughed, appearing not to see the pointed way Carla looked at Marc when she made her last statement. 'She seems to think that she ought to be doing something more positive than she's doing now. Most girls in Hong Kong lead the same kind of life as you do. At least the ones with your background. And so far as all the others are concerned, I wonder if they ought to be working? There are plenty of people in the colony who really need the jobs. Why should the ones who are financially secure take the bread out of their mouths?'

'You can see what kind of life I'm going to have, Marc.' Mr Younger looked at his guest appealingly. 'Two women with moral scruples.'

'Oh?' For an instant Marc looked a bit nonplussed, glancing quickly from his host to Carla and then back again. 'Of course.' He spoke carefully. 'But I imagine you'll be able to hold your own.'

'Well, I'll do my best.' He smiled approvingly at the two women. 'Oh and by the way, you'll know that Joan and I are being married in three weeks' time.' Carla pretended to be absorbed in the design of her coffee cup, refusing to look into Marc's accusing face. 'Is there any chance that you'll be in Hong Kong at the time? We would both love you to come to the wedding.'

'Three weeks?' Marc frowned consideringly while Carla looked at him from beneath her thick dark lashes. 'I'm almost sure that I shan't be, sir. But,' his smile encompassed them both, 'I'm delighted with your news. And of course I offer my best wishes to you both. I think it's the best news I've heard for a long time.'

Mr Younger laughed and looked smugly at Joan. 'I'm inclined to agree with you. But don't tell me that you hadn't heard. I thought that Carla was certain to have told you.' There was the merest shade of reproof in the fond glance he gave his daughter.

'I . . .' She began miserably.

'Of course she did.' Marc interrupted smoothly, studying the end of his cigar before grinding it to extinction in the large crystal ashtray. 'Only,' and his charming smile seemed to envelop them all, even Carla, 'I wasn't quite certain whether it was public knowledge and I didn't want to betray a confidence. You know, on a desert island, although Dalaoa isn't quite that, it is very difficult to keep anything to yourself.' And this time his blatant smile was for Carla alone, full of mocking cynicism. 'Isn't that so, Carla?'

As soon as she could the girl escaped from the small gathering in the saloon who seemed intent on discussing matters which didn't interest her very much. It seemed to be mainly some case which had been receiving a great deal of publicity in Europe where a Swiss drug company was being sued in the courts for a large sum of money following some ill-effects on patients who had used their products. Joan was interested because Mr Younger was, and Colin probably for the same reason. At any other time Carla would have found the discussion stimulating, but tonight she was filled with an aching weariness that seemed to reach to her very soul, banishing her earlier euphoria.

She leaned against the rail of the ship, looking across to the small blob on the starboard that was Dalaoa, thinking of the bungalow and remembering how last night she had lain on the bed waiting for Marc to make love to her. If only . . . If only he had she thought, how different her life would be. And his? she asked herself. Would his have been different too? Would the great experience have changed his opinion for the better? She gave a despondent sigh and raised the glass of tonic water to her lips, then jumped as from the corner of her eye she caught sight of a movement. Knowing it would be him she swung round to face him, seeing the outline of his white clothes against the mahogany super-structure, the dark features looking faintly hawkish and menacing in the moonlight.

'I didn't see you,' she spoke accusingly.

'I'm sorry,' he said unrepentantly and stood watching her.

'Are you going now?' Listlessly she turned away from him, looking down at the black swirling water.

'Yes, I'm going now.' There was a shade of bitter amusement in his voice, but he stepped forward, leaning with one arm on the rail, looking at her. 'Soon you will be rid of me forever.' But then unexpectedly, and Carla had the feeling that he was as surprised at the movement as she was herself, he put out a hand, clasping the back of her neck and turned her round to face him.

At once all her feigned indifference, all her listlessness, all her foolish pretence were swept aside as if a fire consumed her body. She felt herself tremble and knew that he must have been aware of it. As he must have seen her heart hammering beneath the thin covering of silk. Impossible thoughts filled her mind and heart as she wondered if perhaps even now . . . Breathlessly she looked up into the black eyes glittering down at her. She felt the glass which had been suspended over the side of the ship drop from her fingers and strike the water far below.

'You know . . .' And his voice was thoughtful as if he were speaking only to himself, 'I almost regret that last night I allowed my pride to come between us.' His thumb moved sensuously against the tender skin at the nape of her neck. 'It would have been . . . memorable. For me if not for you, *meine schätze*. Yes.' And he sighed. 'There's no doubt that if pride is a sin, then I'm being punished for it now.' His voice was so low that she had to strain to hear it. 'You look so beautiful and so desirable in the moonlight. It's such a pity . . . that I've got to be first. Not just one of a crowd. Goodnight, Carla.' He bent down and brushed her lips with his mouth, turned and strode away from her. And a moment later, she heard the sound of the outboard motor being started, then the faint buzzing as the boat circled the ship and turned for the shore. And Carla stood without moving. Not even aware of the tears glittering like diamonds on her long dark lashes.

CHAPTER TEN

IT felt wonderful to be back in Hong Kong again. Carla knew that if she told herself so often enough she would be convinced. And yet every night when she curled up in bed in the luxurious bedroom on the Peak she thought of that dingy bungalow on Dalaoa, remembered the inconvenience of the outside facilities, the nuisance of cooking without a modern stove and the annoyance of having to read with the aid of a forty-watt bulb.

But in spite of all her endeavours, what seemed more memorable was the lush beauty of the place, the tranquillity of the easy pace of life, of the people she had known there. Deena. She wondered if her cooking was improving. And Asra, the girl who had had the baby. And the baby too. She had been told by the mother that the little boy was to be called Pelmas, a word in the local dialect meaning knife, which doubtless referred to his means of entry into the world. She felt vaguely sad that she would never know what his progress would be. And whether he would have brothers and sisters to join him in the years to come. She shivered a little when she thought of that and hoped that the next child would be able to be born naturally. Otherwise . . . She decided all things considered it was foolish to become sentimental about a remote island. Even she herself hadn't been happy there. It was useless to pretend that she had been.

And what was she now, she asked herself bleakly in

moments of total honesty? Was it any use pretending to herself that in the end the ache in her chest would disappear. For she didn't think she would live that long. And she knew that she would never be able to get Marc Gérard out of her system. Not if she lived to be eighty. Well, maybe by then, she decided with a wry smile at her own stupidity.

In the meantime she was grateful to be caught up in all the stir of the wedding. Grateful too that her father and Joan were too absorbed in themselves to be able to pay too much attention to her. At least so she thought until the day when Joan arrived unexpectedly at the house and surprised Carla in some preparations which she had meant to keep strictly private.

'Hello . . .' After she had consulted Carla about the lists she brought with her Joan picked up the book the girl had been reading, pushing up her spectacles which had slipped to the end of her nose. 'Hello?' She said again, frowned slightly, then gave a quick glance at the spine of the book, '*Modern Nursing Techniques for the SRN*' she read slowly. 'Modern Nursing Techniques,' she repeated in amazement, then took off her glasses and let the book drop from her fingers onto the desk. 'Are these yours, Carla?' She picked up several sheets of paper which were covered with Carla's small neat handwriting.

'Yes.' She had been unprepared for any questions and didn't know how to deal with the matter, only she knew that the colour had drained from her cheeks.

'But . . . but why . . . ?'

'Oh, I just happened to be clearing out and came upon this old manual.' She shrugged, placing the incident into the unimportant, 'You must have known that I took up nursing at one time. But that I couldn't stick it,' she finished bitterly.

'Yes, your father did say something . . .' Joan said slowly. 'But of course he didn't say that you couldn't stick it. He wouldn't believe that and I wouldn't either. Whatever your reasons for giving it up they must have been good ones.'

'Well, they seemed good enough, then.' She tried to speak lightly about it at the same time putting out a hand to relieve Joan of the sheaf of notes she had made earlier. But Joan turned aside, pretending not to see the outstretched hand. 'Now . . .' Her voice trailed away.

'Now,' Joan took up the theme, 'now you're wishing for some reason that you had kept going.'

'Something like that.' The slight laugh was more like a sob, but she managed to capture her property and pushed it along with the book into a drawer with the air of one who meant to change the subject.

'Are you thinking of taking it up again, Carla?' Joan had as always gone to the kernel of the matter, her manner was so subtly sympathetic that Carla all at once felt the need to confide.

'Thinking about it. Yes. You won't tell Daddy, will you, Joan?' She looked anxiously at the older woman. 'Not till I've decided.'

'Not if you don't want me to. Of course I won't.'

'Not yet. Not till I know properly if I can do it. I couldn't bear to let him down again.'

Joan smiled. 'You shouldn't say that, Carla. You haven't let your father down in any way. He would be most upset if he knew you even thought that.'

'Well . . .' She was unconvinced, but unwilling to pursue the matter. 'Just don't say a word to him about it. Only,' she pushed the hair back from her eyes, 'I've got an appointment to see Grace Clemence tomorrow.'

'You mean the matron of the Memorial Hospital?'

'Yes. She and Daddy have been friends for years and I thought I might just as well try to use what influence as I have. Grace doesn't know yet what it's about . . . I want the chance to finish my training. If I can get my SRN then at least I'll feel I've done something on my own.'

'Good for you, love. I know you'll make it.' Joan's confidence was reassuring and sensing that Carla had said all she wanted to at the moment she returned to a discussion of the wedding details. They had more or less finished the seating arrangements when Joan said in a carefully casual voice that brought Carla's head up from her study of the plans.

'Oh and by the way, you did know that Marc Gérard had sent his apologies?'

'No.' Carla bit fiercely at her lips, hoping Joan would not notice the effect her news had had. 'Oh well, he did say it was unlikely.' There was a longish pause. Then, 'How did you hear?'

'Oh Colin, of course. He's been over several times to see about recovering the plane. He took a letter from your father and brought an answer. It arrived this morning and Bob rang me from the office. I'm so sorry, my dear.'

'Sorry?' Carla was indignant. 'What do you mean? Why should you be sorry?'

'I'm just sorry. I was hoping for your sake he'd be here.' A faint smile touched her lips as she looked across the table at the young woman. 'I'm not a fool, Carla. I've seen the way you watch him when you think no-one's looking . . .'

'I don't look at him anyway.' Carla was very busy with her notes. 'I hope you're not going to turn into a match-making Mama.'

'I hope not too.' Joan laughed. 'But I don't think I'm wrong and this decision to try to get back into nursing more or less confirms my opinion.' She looked fondly at the top of the gold head. 'Am I wrong, Carla?'

'No.' It was a long time before the girl answered and although the single word seemed to have been dragged reluctantly from her lips there was a sense of relief as she made the admission. 'No, damn it, you're not wrong. I suppose you'll be satisfied now.' Her voice trembled and tears were ready to flow.

Joan ignored the last words. 'What I can't understand is what is holding the pair of you back.'

'Nothing is holding us back, as you put it.' With an effort Carla regained her self-control and there was even a trace of amusement in her voice. 'Except that Marc can't stand the sight of me.'

'Are you sure of that?'

'Oh, absolutely.' Carla smiled. 'He went out of his way to make certain I got the message. No, there's no chance of a mistake.'

Joan sighed and reached again for one of the lists, 'Well, if you say so, Carla.' Then, with a little laugh, as if regretting that she had brought the matter up, 'and as you say I mustn't turn into a matchmaker. So, if I can ask without being unfairly accused, what about Andrew?'

'Oh, Andy.' Carla smiled and shrugged. 'I think he's

beginning to get the message too. I saw him last night, as you know. We didn't do much, just went with Val Brownlow and Geoff Atkinson to that new Mexican place off Connaught Road. Have you been? No, then I don't know that I'd recommend it, although the floor-show was different. Lots of big hats and cracking whips and some flamenco, which was exciting. But I doubt that Daddy would think much of it.'

'I gather you've decided not to ask Andrew to the wedding after all.'

'No, Daddy doesn't care for him you know and as it's his wedding . . .'

'I'm sure he wouldn't have minded, Carla. Not if you really wanted him to be there.'

'No, I don't. Not particularly. Anyway I've told him it's mainly your friends and Dad's. That's true enough at least, and apart from that I think Andy might be flying home about that time.'

'Well, so long as it's what you want, my dear . . .'

'It's what I want.' Then with an abrupt change of subject which was a direct warning to her future step-mother, 'oh and I've seen a dress that would be just right for the wedding. If you could bring the belt of your outfit Joan, then we could check that the colours don't clash.'

For the rest of the time until the wedding the knowledge that he had refused the invitation lay like a stone against her heart. Although she now accepted that their time had passed there was an almost overwhelming longing, a need to see him. Once or twice when she had been shopping in the crowded market places she had caught sight of a dark head, taller than the rest, making her heart first bound in agitation then drop despairingly when a glimpse revealed the face of a total stranger.

And yet, the very first thing she saw as she entered the church behind Joan and the friend who was giving her away was that unmistakable dark head towering above the others in a pew. She was suddenly so overwhelmed with excitement and nerves, and the small bouquet of cream roses and white heather trembled so obviously that Joan turned to her with a smiling enquiry during the singing of the first hymn. And her own apologetic smile quite concealed the explosion of expectant pleasure which coursed through her veins.

She suddenly felt gloriously alive. As she walked back up the aisle so sedately with her eyes lowered she knew he was watching and when at the last moment she flicked up her eyelids to catch that serious enigmatic expression she had an urge to fight for him, to refuse to let him go without a struggle.

That sense of challenge lasted till the reception at the villa was half-over, and by that time she knew that he had no intention of coming across to speak to her. Even then she had thrust her mounting agitation and disappointment to one side, making up her mind that she would go and find him. But when she went out onto the terrace and looked for him among the guests she saw him bending his head down towards Hélène Veyriet, smiling at whatever she was saying and Hélène was looking up as if she meant to eat him.

And everyone knew what kind of woman she was. Certainly not a shrinking violet if even half of the stories told about her were true. And only tolerated in polite society because her husband Alain was such a poppet. Seeing that he was abandoned to a group of dull old men

Carla changed her mind and went over to speak to him.

Then when the wedding was finally over, when her father and Joan had left for an unknown destination, the house was suddenly empty and very lonely, even the chatter of the girls still clearing things away in the kitchen served only to emphasise the loneliness.

Carla went into her bedroom, listlessly surveyed her reflection in the mirror. It was such a pity to be wearing this beautiful dress and yet to feel so depressed. The pale green material, the small figure-hugging bodice, the flaring skirt, the narrow rouleau belt. All so pretty and yet . . . She turned from the mirror and on impulse threw herself onto the bed.

He hadn't even spoken to her properly. Just goodbye and thank you very much in company with Hélène and Alain. Standing behind them, his eyes had had their usual mesmeric effect, but she had pretended not to notice, saying all the trivial commonplaces a hostess uses on these occasions. But all the time wondering what plans he and Hélène might have for tonight.

There was a sudden tap on her bedroom door and it opened to reveal Jenny, an apologetic expression on her face. 'Sorry, Miss Carla, but someone has come to see you. I told him wait in the drawing-room.'

'Oh all right, Jenny.' She rolled off the bed, looked briefly at her reflection as she walked towards the softly-lit hallway. 'Oh and go as soon as you've finished, Jenny. Just let me know when you get back.'

'Okay, Miss Carla. I'll tell Khim when I go so you won't feel nervous.'

'No, I won't be. You go and have a good time. You've had a lot to do and deserve a night out.'

Without even wondering who the visitor was she walked into the drawing-room, then stopped as he turned from surveying the night lights of Hong Kong from the open windows. Obsessed as she had been with him, somehow the idea that the visitor might be Marc simply hadn't occurred to her.

They stood for a long time looking at each other before she came back to her senses and waved him to a chair. 'How nice to see you. I thought you would have been busy with . . .' The look in his eyes made Hélène's name die on her lips. Biting her lips feverishly she turned away. 'Would you like a drink?'

'No. No thanks.' He shook his head abruptly and one hand which had been in the pocket of his jacket pulled out a small packet. 'I brought you these.' He held it out towards her. 'You left them in the drawer in the bungalow.'

'Oh.' With admirable restraint she controlled the trembling of her fingers as she opened the envelope and was not surprised to find the earrings she had been wearing when the plane had crashed. 'You shouldn't have troubled.' How ungracious she was sounding. As if those plans to fight for him had never been made. 'There was no need to come back specially.'

'It was no trouble.' He was tight-lipped and laconic as ever. 'I simply wanted to make sure they reached you safely.'

'Oh, they're not valuable. Only costume jewellery.'

'Nevertheless . . .'

'Well,' at last she looked directly at him, willing herself to find him different, unattractive, all his appeal for her gone. But the insistent beating of her heart told her that nothing had changed, that she loved him with the same wild desperation, even as he held her in the same cold disdain, 'Would you like a cup of tea, coffee?'

'No thanks.' He glanced at the heavy gold watch on his wrist, shooting back the white cuff so that she had a momentary glimpse of the slender fingers, remembered their delicate touch as he pulled a new life into the world. 'I think I had . . .'

But before he had time to make his goodbyes there was a murmur of voices in the hallway, Jenny opened the door and announced, 'Miss Clemence', and a tall impressive woman with firmly waved iron grey hair came into the room.

'Ah, Carla,' her quick glance towards the man who stood with his back to the windows showed no sign of recognition, 'I'm so pleased I caught you, my dear.'

'Oh, Grace.' At the moment the matron of the Memorial Hospital was the last person she wished to see, but some kind of introduction was inevitable. 'Grace, this is . . . Marc Gérard, Miss Grace Clemence.' Polite murmurs emanated from both visitors and Grace refused the invitation to sit down.

'No, I mustn't, Carla. I happened to be passing with the Osbornes and I asked them to stop at the gate. They're giving me a lift to a reception at the Governor's tonight. Oh, by the way, how did the wedding go?'

'Very well, I think. They left about two hours ago.'

'I'm so pleased. I think they're ideally suited to each other, don't you?'

'Yes.' Carla was growing more and more conscious of the silent figure on her right. 'Yes, I'm sure they'll be

happy. I'm pleased.' She made the admission for the first
time.

'Good. I just thought I'd let you know everything's
arranged and I've brought you these forms.' She took
some folded papers from her bag and placed them on the
table before turning with a nod in Marc's direction.
'Well goodnight, Mr Gérard. Nice to have met you.' She
went towards the door with Carla trailing behind her.
'Then, we'll see you on Tuesday, Carla. I know you want
to get started as soon as possible. Don't forget to bring
the completed forms with you. And report to Sister
Evans.' Carla pulled the door of the drawing-room,
hoping that the sound of its closing would drown Matron's rather penetrating voice. 'It's not often I go out of
my way to do this, Carla. But I was always very fond of
your parents and I know you'll make a fine nurse.'

When the front door had closed behind her Carla
stood for a moment looking at it before turning slowly.
And there standing in the open door of the drawing-
room, the door she had closed seconds earlier, and with
an expression on his face which told her he had heard
every word of the conversation, stood Marc Gérard. The
calmness of her face as she walked the few steps towards
him was wholly assumed, concealing the desperation she
now felt. She must get rid of him. At once. Before she
broke down completely.

'Well, if you *must* be off,' she said pointedly and was
disconcerted when he turned back towards the room,
holding the door open so that she had no choice but to
precede him, to watch while he closed the door and came
towards her. Feeling that her legs would soon give way
beneath her she sank into a chair then gasped when she

saw Marc's hand reach out to pick up the fold of papers from the table.

'These are personal.' It was not a very brilliant protest and did nothing to stop his swift perusal of the papers which he returned almost at once.

'So,' the mouth twisted in what might have been meant as a smile, the dark eyes were as penetrating as ever, 'You mean to become a nurse after all? What's wrong, do you find all this boring?' As he half-turned to indicate the luxurious surroundings, his eyes never released hers, but Carla was wounded by the hint of sarcasm.

'I wouldn't expect you to understand.' A deep unhappy sigh shuddered through her body and she managed to wrench her eyes away from his. 'Whatever I do you will be sure to find some shameful reason for it.' Deliberately she forced herself from the chair and, ignoring him, walked over to the open window, trying not to notice the dark shadowy presence at her elbow. 'But if it will give you any satisfaction, then I'll admit it. Yes, I do find it a bit boring.'

'And what makes you think that this time you'll be able to stay the course? What's so different now?'

Anger suddenly flared in her, momentarily driving out the misery which was caused even more by his presence than his absence. 'Why should I explain anything to you? You wouldn't understand.' She whirled round to face him challengingly. 'Ever since we first met you've gone out of your way to show me how much you dislike and despise me.'

'Is that what you think, Carla?' He spoke her name tenderly, at the same time putting out a finger to touch

her cheek. 'Do you really believe that? I thought . . .' his
finger trickled seductively against her skin, '. . . once or
twice I thought that I had given some very firm indication that I . . . didn't dislike you that much.'

Carla had to fight the torment his touch was bringing,
the weakness that inclined her to put her hand over his,
to hold his fingers still closer against her face. Passionate
attack was the only weapon she had at her disposal. She
chose to ignore his reference to the emotions that had
flared between them back on the island but returned to
his earlier charge. 'I think I'll be able to stay the course,
that's what you said wasn't it? I think I'll be able to stick
it because I'm a different person. And because the
circumstances are different. I should have thought you
would be pleased,' something very like a sob escaped her
lips, 'instead of always being so keen to criticise.'

'Circumstances different?' In the half-dark she sensed
a derisively raised eyebrow, longed to move away from
his touch, but would not give him the satisfaction of
knowing how much it disturbed her. 'How, Carla? Tell
me.' His voice was gentle, persuasive, as if he really
wanted to know and suddenly she felt all the anger ease
away from her. And it had nothing to do with the way his
fingers had circled her neck, how they were moving
delicately against her nape, nor how he was pulling her
closer to him, so that she felt his breath on her face. 'Tell
me, Carla.'

'Because,' her shuddering sob was stifled against the
smooth cloth of his jacket, tears forced themselves
between closed lids and gratefully she took the folded
handkerchief which he put into her hand. 'Because,' she
sobbed, 'I was so unhappy then.'

'And now, *meine schätze*,' his voice was full of delight-ed amusement, 'you are so happy? Hmm?' His cheek came down and rested for a moment against her hair and Carla discovered all sorts of wild feelings surging within her, the feelings that she had vowed to put away from her for ever. 'So happy that you think to become a nurse will be easy.'

Much of this Carla chose to ignore, going to what she considered the essentials. 'What did you call me?' She leaned away from him, wiped her face with the handker-chief, blowing her nose in a very unromantic way as she looked up.

'I called you *meine schätze*. You know what that means?'

She shook her head, or at least began to before his hands pulling her closer to him put a stop to all her defiance. She felt her body being moulded against his, his mouth against her cheeks, her eyes, was murmuring her name as if he would never stop. And only when his lips closed on hers, when he took her on a mind-spinning star-spangled trip to somewhere close to Paradise did the sound of his voice cease.

At last, after a long time they drifted back to earth, settling dreamily as they gazed at each other bemusedly. 'Carla.' He spoke her name again, lingeringly with just that faint accent which would always be able to stir her senses. '*Ich liebe dich. Ich liebe dich.*'

'And what,' she asked huskily, dreamily, deviously, 'does that mean?'

'You know too well what it means. You know, have known from the beginning. And I'm going to spend a long time convincing you, telling you in every language that I know. But first, Carla,' his hands came up to cradle her face, 'tell me what I have to know. What made you so unhappy all those years ago? So unhappy that you gave up nursing?'

She put her head back against his chest, preferring to tell the story without his perceptive eyes so constantly on hers. 'You see, I had never really thought of being a nurse. Not till my mother died, and then I suddenly thought it was the only possible life for me. Daddy didn't think it was a good idea, but you know me,' she shrugged apologetically, 'spoiled, determined to have my own way. Anyway I managed to get into a first class hospital to do my training and slowly I began to get over what had happened, to make new friends.' She sighed and he waited patiently for her to continue. 'And then I met someone, a doctor at the hospital and . . .' she hesitated.

'And he fell in love with you?' he prompted gently.

'I think we fell in love with each other.' She reached up a hand to touch his cheek. 'Do you mind, Marc?'

'Of course I mind. But I understand. Go on, Carla.'

'And then, he had to go into hospital for some tests, then immediate surgery. Oh, Marc.' While she sobbed he held her firmly stroking her head and murmuring comfortingly till she regained control. 'Hamish died just six weeks after he first noticed something was wrong. He, he had tried to make me accept my mother's suffering and death. Then he was gone. I couldn't bear it. I just left and came home. I never told Daddy. I didn't want to open up the old wounds. I think maybe he suspected I'd had an unhappy love affair, but he didn't know why.'

He held her till her sobbing eased. 'Oh Carla.' His sigh

was filled with regret. 'You should have told your father. Isn't that what families are for, to comfort each other, to *help* each other when life becomes impossible?' For a long time no-one spoke, then at last, 'You think now Carla that you will be able to take it all, the hard work, the studying? The pain when you find that you can't save one of your patients.'

'I'm going to do it,' she stated with firm assurance. 'Other people can. I'm going to do it.'

'And,' he put a finger under her chin, tilted her head back and looked gravely down at her, 'where do I come into the plans you have for the future.'

'I . . . I . . .' She shook her head, unable to think of anything but the dazzling possibilities which now seemed worth considering. 'I don't know what you mean.'

'Oh come.' He laughed gently, confidently. 'You must have some idea why I'm here. Why I had to come back to see you. Why I *forgot* to leave your earrings when I came to the wedding this afternoon.'

Now it was her turn to demand an explanation, simply because she knew that she would explode if he postponed it any longer. She didn't even waste time by teasing him about his confession that he could have left the earrings earlier if he had wanted to. 'Why, why did you have to come back?'

'For this.' He dropped a kiss on her lips. 'And this.' His mouth tantalised hers. 'And simply because,' he said at last, 'I couldn't keep away.' Under her ears his heart was beating with fierce impatience.

'But Hélène,' she murmured dreamily. 'I thought you and she . . .'

'This afternoon, I forced myself to stay with her. But all the time it was you I was watching. Seeing you look so beautiful in your bridesmaid's dress, knowing that there was only one cure for this serious condition I've at last diagnosed.'

'And that is?' To help him to come to a speedy conclusion she slipped her hand under the thin jacket, felt the contours of his body through the silk shirt.

'I decided that there was no help for it, I would have to marry you.'

'I wish,' she laughed softly then drew his head down to hers, 'I wish you didn't sound so reluctant.'

'I'm not.' He swung her round, off her feet. 'I'm more sure of this than of anything that happened to me before. In spite of all the ups and downs . . .'

'Ups and down . . .' She sighed. 'Surely no-one has had to endure so many as we have. Why Marc? Why were you such a *brute*?'

'I suppose,' after a long, impossibly sweet interlude he went on, 'I suppose the only excuse I can offer is that since I first saw you that evening in Macao I've been in a state of shock. You see, I recognised you that first moment, the girl I had been looking for all my life. Then, it seemed you had a husband in tow. And maybe a drink problem.'

'A drink problem?' Indignation flashed between them as she looked up so that he dropped a conciliatory kiss on her forehead. 'How could you think such . . .' Then the scene returned to her mind, she remembered the struggle in the hotel corridor, the spilt whisky. 'But then,' she moved to a less logical attacking point, pouted, feeling deliciously frail and feminine, 'then you had to go and put your foot in it with Daddy. You were so *mean*. And enjoyed it so much.'

'It's a way I have.' He put back his head and laughed. 'You'll have to try to convert me. But that night did seem to confirm you were having an *affaire* with Andrew. That's what's been bugging me most of all. That's what had me inventing good reasons for deciding there could be nothing between us. First you were married. And if you weren't then you went around having casual affaires. After that it was easy enough. You were the daughter of a millionaire, a social gadfly who would never think of marrying an ordinary doctor. Then that you had no staying power.'

'I hope I've explained that.' It was delight to brush her mouth against his as she spoke. 'And I've never had affaires, casual or otherwise.'

'I'm glad.' His voice was husky. 'And I hope you're going to answer my question soon.'

'What question was that?' she whispered, anxious only that he should repeat it.

'I asked you to marry me. Soon Carla. We've wasted so much time.'

'Soon,' she agreed in a state of intoxication. 'When I've finished at the Memorial. In about six months' time, if I work hard, then . . .'

'Six months.' His arms tightened till they threatened her breathing. 'I can't wait six months.' Urgent and forceful as he was she had to hang onto some remnants of her resolve.

'And what makes you think that marriage won't occupy me so much that I'll throw it all up again? The nursing I mean.'

'I don't know.' He sounded faintly distraught. 'I don't even seem to care any more.'

'You know,' she teased, 'the matron where I began my training said I had the makings of a first-class nurse, can you believe that, Marc?'

'Yes, I can believe it. Easily.' He gave the impression of having his mind very much on something else. 'But when shall we get married, Carla?'

'I've just had this idea.' She linked her hands about his neck and arched her body provocatively against his. 'This idea of mine could just solve the whole problem. When do you have to go back to Dalaoa?'

'Oh I don't know.' Distractedly he raked a hand through his hair. 'Tuesday, Wednesday. It doesn't matter really. If only we could get this settled.'

'That reminds me. That night when you were being so mean to me. At the party here, you said that when you weren't there your patients simply died. That was a moment before you accused me of having a dress that would have kept them all in food for a hundred years.'

'Yes.' He almost groaned. 'I was a pompous ass. Forgive me. I would have said anything to try to convince myself that you weren't the girl I wanted you to be. In fact they are ridiculously healthy on Dalaoa and my work is more concerned with research than anything else. The little I have to do as far as health care goes is just an extra. Forgive me, my darling. I was trying to let you know how important I was.'

Her manner seemed to show him how completely he was forgiven and it was some time before he remembered to ask her about the idea she had had.

'You see, I've just thought that as you're to be in Hong

Kong till after I start at the Memorial, then there's no reason why you shouldn't stay here. There is a spare room which is reasonably comfortable and if you find that it isn't up to the required standard you can . . .' She pulled his head close enough for him to hear her whispered suggestion.

'You mean . . .' In the half-dark his eyes blazed down at her although his voice was unusually humble. 'You're sure, darling.'

'Quite, quite sure.' She sighed and lay for a moment with her cheek against his hammering pulses. 'And then,' she stretched comfortably, standing on tiptoe and reaching her arms about his neck, 'in between times you could coach me.'

'Coach you?' He laughed softly, causing ripples of excitement to trickle down her spine, 'what subjects had you in mind, Carla?'

'Marc!' She felt her cheeks grow warm. 'Well all sorts of things I hope. But what I really meant was that you should coach me in all the kinds of things an SRN should know.'

'That, my sweet, is exactly what I had in mind. If we really work at it you should be able to pick up a great deal before Tuesday. Don't you agree?'